Acclaim for Thomas Longfellow's

GUARDIANS OF THE GIFT

"A politically conflicted nation faces internal dissent and the threat of invasion in Longfellow's fast-paced allegorical novel of dystopian fantasy."

-Kirkus Reviews

"Must read page turner! Guardians of the Gift grabs you by the throat in the first chapter and never lets go. The multiple storylines all come together in the last few chapters."

-Maria V.

"Longfellow's masterpiece has everything--action, adventure, political philosophy, and solid character development. It allegorizes the principles of America and interprets the definition of freedom in a whole new light."

-Zachary T.

Guardians of the Gift

Thomas Longfellow

Contact the author: Guardiansofthegift@gmail.com
Website: www.Guardiansofthegift.com

Historical Map – 243 Years Ago

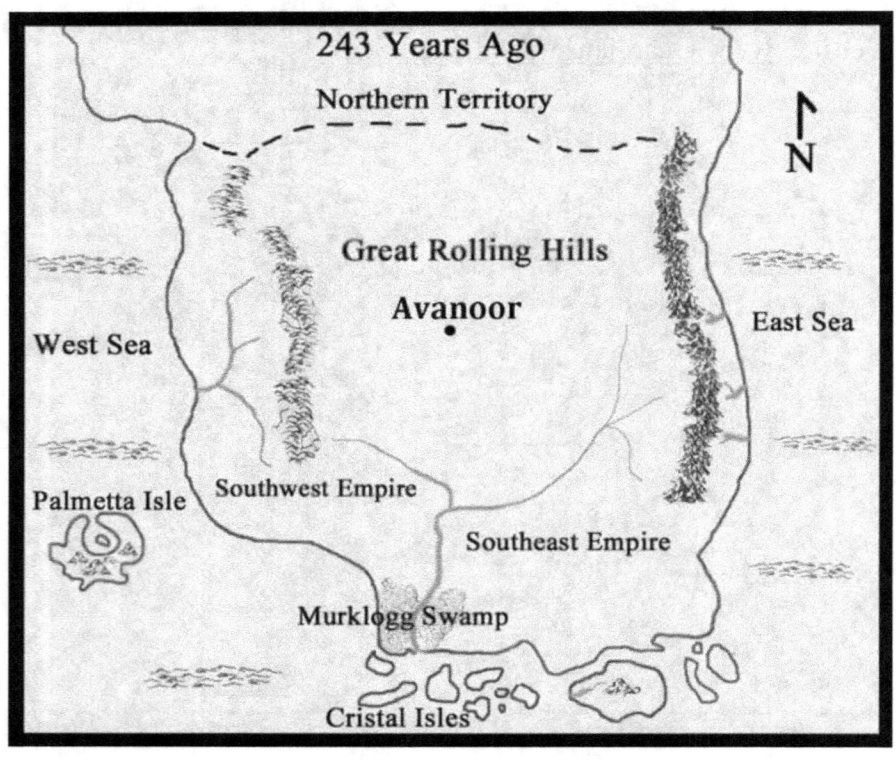

The Current Era

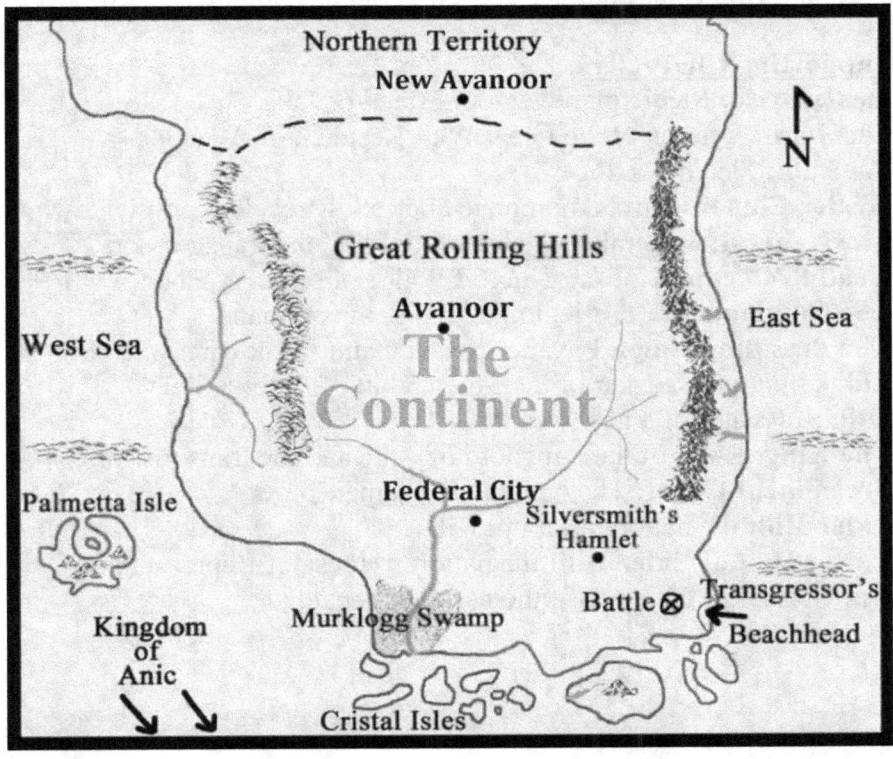

Character List

Main Characters:
Thomas Longfellow: Silversmith
Head Protector Willard Gallatae: Avanoor Chief of Police
Healer Jake Gallatae: Medic in the legion. Son of Willard Gallatae
Healer Jenny Gallatae: Resident physician. Daughter of Willard
Fletcher Gallatae: Founder of New Avanoor. Son of Willard

Supporting Characters:
Healer Arlo: Medic in the legion. Friend of Jake.
Old John: Veteran of the Great War. Resident of Avanoor
Winston: Fletcher's dog
Healer Chloe: Jenny's roommate and fellow resident physician
The General: General of the legion fighting the transgressors
Head Protector Kinton: Chief of Police of New Avanoor
The Commander: The legion's second in command
The Presiding Chief: President of the nation. Known as the "PC"
Elder Bertha: Speaker of the Lower Half of Elder Hill
Sofia: Inventor of a new weapon
The King: Ruler of the Kingdom of Anic and the transgressors
Preeminent Court: The nation's Supreme Court
Elder Hill: the nation's Capitol Hill
Lower Half of Elder Hill: the nation's House of Representatives
Upper Half of Elder Hill: the nation's Senate

Prologue

The first five chapters of this book introduce the main characters and their storylines. Their destinies are unknowingly intertwined in the nation's struggle for survival. Four of the main characters are related.

Chapter 1 introduces Thomas Longfellow who lives in a small hamlet. Thomas is a silversmith nearing the successful completion of his apprenticeship. Also, "Thomas Longfellow" is the pen name of the author. The author and the character in this book are not the same individual. The author apologizes for any confusion. It's his first novel and he appreciates the readers' understanding for this rookie misstep.

Chapter 2 introduces Healer Jake who is a medic on the frontlines of battle fighting an invading horde in the southeast. The following character, Willard, is his father.

Chapter 3 introduces Willard Gallatae who is the chief of police (known as the Head Protector) of a village named Avanoor. Willard is the father of Healer Jake and the following two characters—Jenny and Fletcher.

Chapter 4 introduces Jenny who recently finished medical school and moved to the capital of the nation (known as Federal City) to start her medical residency.

Finally, Chapter 5 introduces Fletcher who is the elder brother to Jake and Jenny. Fletcher pioneered a new settlement in the northern frontier called New Avanoor.

The map on the preceeding page shows the corresponding locations of each of the main characters.

Introduction

Over 240 years ago, in a distant land from a long forgotten era, a small village—known as Avanoor—faced extinction.

Centrally located on a massive expanse of territory known simply as the Continent, Avanoor was a peaceful tribe of a few hundred rudimentary farmers.

The story of Avanoor began on a frigid winter night.

Escaping the unendurable conditions of the Northern Territory, bands of savages fled south into the Great Rolling Hills to plunder the many Grasslander tribes for food and women and to quench their thirst for blood.

The events of that night thrusted the entire world into a new era.

During the following winter months the tribes of the Great Rolling Hills united, defeated the savages, and unintentionally founded a vibrant new civilization. Over the following decades it burgeoned throughout the Continent, defeated the tyrannical southern empires, and united all peoples.

The Continent experienced a level of peace and prosperity unimaginable to any human that lived prior to the Savage War. Each generation continued the tradition of freedom, liberty, and prosperity. They repelled foreign invaders from their shores. They achieved inconceivable advancements in farming resulting in abundant food surpluses. The average human in each subsequent generation lived a longer, healthier, and more comfortable life than the previous generations.

After two centuries of defending their nation from barbaric armies they faced a new danger—a threat from within.

The nine High Priests in the Preeminent Court upheld a newly passed law—Right to a Healer. The Chief Priest granted the federal government nearly unlimited power to compel citizens to engage in commerce through Elder Hill's constitutional power to tax.

A decade later and after fiscal belt-tightening decimated the nation's military strength, the Continent's incredible wealth was no longer the singular force beckoning the attention of a rapacious foreign empire.

That is where this story begins.

Chapter 1

Four years ago, on a scorching summer day during the pork boom of the Southeast, a hog farmer and his son cleared rocks and boulders from a parcel of their land adjacent to a river. The ten year old boy carried home a brick-sized stone that was slightly different from the others.

After weeks of clearing rocks out of forty acres of land, the father developed a deep abhorrence for the agonizing obstructions on his fertile fields. The son and mother quickly tired of the father's never-ending cursing.

Darn worthless boulders goin' to break my back. I prefer a dang cloud o' crop eatin' bugs.

The father cringed every time he saw his son's brick-sized souvenir from the riverbank. The father wanted it discarded in the river with the other stones. The mother refused to let the boy take the unusually heavy rock—caked with dry mud—inside her house. However, the son persisted. He wouldn't give up his new treasure.

The family found compromise.

For over a year it was the home's doorstop until the neighbor tripped over it and realized it wasn't just a stone. He disclosed to the family the doorstop's true identity.

The neighbor—a former prospector—and the father soon discovered that the river's bottom was carpeted in gold nuggets. They managed to keep it a secret for only a year.

The Southeast, once known for plentiful pork and bountiful bacon, was reborn as the Continent's new wealth engine—the Southern Gold Rush. The Federal treasury's hunger for gold bars was insatiable. The elites' unquenchable thirst for ornate gems and finely crafted gold and silver adornment drove the Continent's jewelry market.

Over the following three years this immense demand for the precious metals pulsated straight through a small quiet hamlet on the trade route between the Southeast and Federal City—Thomas Longfellow's home town.

His father, the Continent's renowned silversmith, owned a thriving business that was both a silver shop and a precious metals trading post. As the eldest son, Thomas's seven year silversmith apprenticeship was nearly complete. His three younger brothers were not far behind.

Elites, Federals, and elders craved Longfellow's finely crafted metallic art. No other silversmith could compete with the quality. The finely scripted "LF" trademark was found on every Longfellow masterpiece. It was a mark of luxury, honor, and prestige.

The twenty-seven year old Thomas Longfellow eagerly looked forward to assisting his father expand the family business. He dreamt of a lifelong career following in his father's footsteps.

However, fate had other plans.

The sun slid below the horizon. Thomas's father and three brothers were enjoying dinner with the chief of their hamlet. It was Thomas's turn to close shop and shoo off the line of miners and traders eager to do business.

However, on this evening, there weren't many prospectors to disperse. The lines had significantly dwindled from previous nights. Thomas assumed the heavy monsoon to the south caused a temporary lull in business.

He didn't mind the decreased business—it'd be a nice break. The shop operated six days a week from sunrise to sunset. A grueling work ethic and pride in his jewelry—not profits—drove his father.

The federal government's "profit quotas" removed any incentive for the Longfellows to work more than three hours each day. The family of silversmiths reached their daily profit quota well before lunch. The Federals collected any profit made after the Longfellows met their daily quota.

Thomas's father was one of the few small business owners in the region that didn't let the profit quota dilute his work ethic.

Cleaning the shop and snuffing a few candles stood in the way of Thomas's dinner. He shooed off a couple loitering traders outside and paused when he was an arm's length from the shop's front door.

Thomas thought he heard the faint sound of hooves trotting on the worn stone road. He squinted in the fading twilight. The rare noise came from the south. His eyes focused on a horse over a hundred paces away on the road. The creature turned off the trade route and headed towards Longfellow's shop.

He squinted again. A man was slumped on the horse. His arms dangled to the side. The horse guided itself. Two long sticks protruded from the rider's back.

Strange.

The horse trotted straight for Longfellow.

What in God's name?

The horse slowed. Longfellow could see colors—blood, two arrows, and the look of death.

He cupped his hands over his mouth—the smell of death.

The horse stopped one pace in front of Thomas. He grabbed the loose reins and cautiously stepped towards the bloodied figure.

He's a legionnaire?!

Longfellow's mind raced. A hundred questions flashed through his head.

Is he alive? What's he doing here? Was he robbed by thugs? Why didn't anyone see him on the road? Those arrows look foreign.

The bloodied legionnaire moaned. Thomas jumped back.

Alive!? What do I do? There's no healer here. The hamlet isn't large enough to qualify for one. My sister...

Longfellow said, "Hang on, my little sister is home from healer school—"

The dying man wheezed, "No, stay here. What...what is your name?"

"Ahh, Thomas Longfellow. Sir, you need medical care. My sister—"

Blood seeped out of the corners of his mouth.

He coughed, "What is your profession?"

4

"Ahh, sir?"

The rider's bloodied hand gripped Thomas's shoulder. Shocked at the legionnaire's stength, Thomas winced in pain.

The rider repeated himself, "What do you do? Your job?"

Longfellow answered, "Sir, I'm a silversmith."

"Your father?"

"Silversmith."

"Grandfather?"

"Died in the Great War. My father never met his own—"

"Did you serve in the legion?"

Longfellow's eyes focused on the blood splattered gold rope around the legionnaire's upper arm.

"Ah, yes sir. For three years. You're a commander's aide? What are you doing—?"

The rider released Thomas's shoulder.

"What..." the legionnaire coughed more blood, "what do you think of the Enlightened?"

Confusion gripped Longfellow's face.

Why is a dying commander's aide, with arrows in his back, asking me about the Enlightened?

Blood dripped off the rider's chin onto the back of the horse's neck. The legionnaire's hand clamped Longfellow's shoulder again. He squeezed.

Thomas winced, "Ahh, the Enlightened. I don't know. I just make silverware."

The legionnaire sighed in relief. Blood gurgled in his throat.

Skirting that question was the standard response from Heartless. Publicly criticizing the Enlightened wasn't illegal, but was risky. Heartless played it safe by dancing around the question. Fellow Enlightened and moderate Traditionalists answered with lavish praise for the Presiding Chief and his social programs.

However, the rider was unsure if Thomas would surrender his profession, his dreams, and possibly his life to deliver a message.

The legionnaire hacked up more blood. His vision grayed. His hand still rested on Longfellow's shoulder. The rider's piercing eyes hooked the silversmith's attention.

The rider said, "You must heed each word I say. The Continent is under attack. Those arrows are from the Kingdom of Anic. They will be here in a matter of days. There's not much time, you have to—"

Thomas shook his head in disbelief, "No, no, the General of our legion traveled through a week or two ago. He purchased jewelry from us. He himself told us that the transgressors were subdued."

The legionnaire shook Thomas and snarled, "Look at my back! Look at those arrows. Does that look subdued?"

The bloodied rider, slowly succumbing to death, had no time. Longfellow was his only hope.

His grip on Longfellow's shoulder weakened. His eyelids struggled to remain cracked open. With little remaining strength in his muscles, he reached into a leather pouch and withdrew a sealed letter.

The rider handed Thomas the note and said, "Unseal and read this. Deliver it to the head protector of Avanoor—Willard Gallatae. Your hamlet, the Continent, and tens of thousands of lives depend on it."

Thomas asked, "Avanoor…the historic Avanoor?"

"Avanoor of our history, Avanoor of Servius, Crassius, and Kamila. Take my horse and go now."

"But you need medical attention, my sister is—"

"There is no time for me. Take my horse. And snap one of the arrows from my back as proof. Go now!"

With his last ounce of energy, the legionnaire pushed himself off the horse. His body crashed to the ground. His eyes closed.

Thomas leaned over—his ear inches from the rider's mouth. He barely heard the legionnaire's faint breath.

Still alive.

"Stay with me, sir."

He dragged the dying legionnaire around the shop to the back. He stopped at the entrance of the tool shed. Thomas opened the door, leaned over, grabbed the rider's arms, and pulled him into the shed.

Thomas said, "Come on, don't die. I need—"

The rider's eyes flashed open.

He reached up, grabbed Thomas's collar with one hand, and said "Legionnaire. You took an oath to protect the Document. It will be burned if you don't get on that horse and go now. That is your sworn duty."

6

Thomas froze. Those words pierced his heart and awoke forgotten memories. He hasn't been called a legionnaire for seven years.

His mind replayed the morning he took the oath a decade ago—the day he was initiated into that sacred brotherhood.

Taking the oath was the culmination of two months of agonizing training in the western mountain range. Marching through icy rain and mountain snow during the night built discipline. Suffering from deficient sleep and a meager calorie intake, the recruits burned their daylight hours on the archery range, conducted unceasing sword fighting, and tackled the academics of battlefield maneuvering. Each recruit learned how the mind could push the body well beyond the limits of their perceived physical capabilities.

The final test was a thirty hour hump, in full battle gear, to the summit of a mountain overlooking the Great Rolling Hills.

After scaling the peak during the night's ice storm, Thomas and nineteen other recruits and their cadre arrived at the summit in the early morning. The gray overcast sky shielded the frozen mountains and plains from the warm sun. The cadre lined the twenty shivering and physically depleted men facing the expansive view of the Great Rolling Hills. A biting gust of wind stung their faces. The twenty frigid recruits raised their right hands.

Halfway through the oath, a ray of sun punched through a small break in the clouds and painted the men in fresh brilliance. It warmed more than Longfellow's skin.

That moment seared into Longfellow's mind—the words, the warmth, and the view of the Continent.

After saying the words "So help me God" Longfellow was charged with the duty to protect the Document from all enemies—foreign and domestic.

Thomas Longfellow snapped himself out of his reverie. He returned to reality.

He looked at the bloodied rider lying inside the shed. He bent over and felt for a pulse in his neck and both wrists.

Nothing.

He placed his ear next to the man's mouth.

Nothing.

The legionnaire had passed onto the other world.

Longfellow panicked. He left the shed and darted into the shop. He unsealed the note, held it under the candle light, and read it.

He read it a second time.

If this is true, God save us all.

Longfellow's mind raced. Fear poured into his heart. Uncertainty clouded his judgment.

The pitch black of night had arrived. His father and brothers would return within the hour.

Doubt and anxiety reverberated through his body.

He illegally possessed a horse. A dead legionnaire rested in his father's tool shed. In his hand was a note. If true, the transgressors from the Kingdom of Anic would sack his peaceful hamlet in the next few days and probably kill everyone.

Confusion and ambiguity blurred his mind.

The recent lull in business…it's not due to the monsoon.

He returned to the tool shed holding a candle. He stepped inside. The candle light illuminated the cluttered wood shack. He looked down at the dead legionnaire.

Longfellow's eyes focused on the flag—a patch sewn onto the uniform. A familiar warmth raced through his body.

His thoughts rebounded back to the day he took the oath—the day he received his flag. Recruits weren't authorized to wear the symbolic patch. They had to earn the title of "legionnaire" and swear to protect the Document first.

He thought of the frigid mountain summit. He recalled shivering, holding his right hand up, and peering down on the Continent. The ray of light that broke through the clouds wasn't from the sun.

The sun can't warm one's soul.

The dormant legionnaire inside of him awoke.

Others over self.

Longfellow's mind cleared.

Focus. Commitment. Strength. Confidence. Courage. Honor.

Adrenaline pulsed through his veins. He leaned over the legionnaire's corpse. He snapped one of the arrows off his back. He ran into the silver shop and folded the note. He held a bar of red wax up to the candle. He dripped it over the broken seal on the folded note. He stamped the Longfellow seal into the molten wax.

L.F.

The front door of the shop creaked open. Longfellow looked up. His sister peeked inside.

She said, "I figured you'd still be here. Why is there a horse—?"

Her eyes converged onto his candle lit face.

"Thomas, are you alright?"

He replied, "Pack your bags."

Chapter 2

Three Weeks Earlier

"To put, in place of the delegated will of the Nation, the will of a party; often a small but artful and enterprising minority of the Community... They are likely, in the course of time and things, to become potent engines, by which cunning, ambitious, and unprincipled men will be enabled to subvert the Power of the People and to usurp for themselves the reins of Government; destroying afterwards the very engines which have lifted them to unjust dominion...is itself a frightful despotism. But this leads at length to a more formal and permanent despotism. The spirit of encroachment tends to consolidate the powers of all the departments in one, and thus to create whatever form of government, a real despotism."
George Washington – Farewell Address, September 1796

The Southeast Region of the Continent

Dense rain cascaded from the dark sky. Thunder rumbled the drenched earth. The ominous ceiling of clouds radiated with lightning. The torrential rain slamming into the ground muffled the sounds of battle. The rainy season in the Southeast had begun.

Healer Jake stood inside a large hospital tent shielded from the rain. His hand rested on the friar's shoulder. Dark rings hung below their eyes. Their uniforms were bloodied and unkempt. Jake leaned towards the friar's ear.

He whispered, "Friar, these three won't...won't—"

The friar whispered, "I understand. Is it safe?"

"Yes, the boss is sleeping. I'll keep an eye open for him."

The friar nodded and walked to the first of the three souls who were on the verge of leaving their human bodies. Jake couldn't watch. He headed to the exit of the healer tent. He hesitated before stepping outside into the downpour. He turned around for one last glance and watched the friar take a knee at the first man lying on a cot. The friar rested his hand on the forehead of the dying legionnaire.

Jake closed his eyes and lowered his head. He tried swallowing to soothe the lump in his throat. It only grew tighter. He looked back at the other two men taking their final breaths.

He held himself together for nearly two straight days with no sleep. The sight of his fellow legionnaires leaving this world tore at his soul. He didn't recognize some, but many were close friends and classmates. All were his brothers in arms. Seventeen faces of the men who died while under his care in the previous hours raced through his mind. Three more would soon join his living nightmare.

He glanced around the tent at the four dozen wounded men still alive. They would live. However, he took little solace that his team saved many lives in that tent. He wished he could save them all. One life lost was too many. His team of healers did everything in their power to save those who perished, but it wasn't enough. It would never be enough.

The friar lightly stepped over to the second legionnaire. He took a knee.

Jake turned back to the slit in the tent. He forced himself to step outside. He walked out into the deluge. He looked up into the cool rain. It sliced through the wall of humidity. The downpour rinsed the sweat, blood, and grime off his face. He took a deep breath.

Someone interrupted his short moment of peace.

"Healer Jake! Healer Jake!"

He looked to his left. The messenger ran towards him through the monsoon.

"Healer Jake, you're needed in the prisoner's hospital tent!"

Jake understood. He didn't hesitate. He ran towards the prisoner tent with the messenger. Puzzled about the source of his energy, he sprinted past the rows of drenched white sheets covering the bodies of his fallen legionnaires. He didn't look. He couldn't look. Outside the prisoner tent were more bodies—enemy bodies. He watched as a half-dozen legionnaires carried more bodies from the battlefield.

Jake shook his head.

These weren't transgressors. More like invaders.

He pushed aside the flap covering the tent's opening. He stepped inside. Water streamed off Jake's chin. The soaked messenger ducked into the tent behind him.

Jake saw his friend, Healer Arlo, standing over a transgressor. His hands pressed over a wound in the abdomen. Blood seeped out around Arlo's fingers.

"Jake, I need some help over here."

Jake had seen that wound enough today.

He replied, "Arlo, he's not going to make it."

It wasn't his code to let people die without trying. But there was nothing he could do to save him. He walked up to the dying transgressor.

He's just a kid. Probably no more than fourteen years old.

Fear streamed out from the kid's wide open eyes. He tried to breathe. He coughed blood. His body shivered.

Jake asked, "Where's the leaf?"

Arlo's hands remained pressed against the kid's wound. The kid's hand tightly gripped Arlo's wrist. It was his soul's physical attempt to cling onto life.

Jake and Arlo looked down at the dying transgressor. They didn't want the kid to let go. But the leaf didn't save lives. It was to put them at ease. Arlo nodded in agreement with Jake. The messenger carried over a wood bowl of green paste. Arlo lifted his hands exposing the kid's wound.

Jake scooped out a handful of the dark green paste. He could smell the ground leaf's cool sweet odor as he applied it onto the open wound. The kid's body stopped shivering. His contorted face relaxed. His eyes began emanating peace. The kid loosened his grip on Arlo's wrist.

Jake whispered to the kid, "This will stop the pain."

The kid nodded. His eyes slowly closed. All of his muscles relaxed. His head fell back.

Jake looked into the eyes of Arlo and the messenger. He could see their tortured souls. No man was immune to this horror. Jake looked back down at the kid's lifeless body.

Jake placed his hand over the young boy's face and closed his eyes.

He's just a kid. May God take mercy on his soul.

Jake looked back up. Another death. Another face in his nightmares.

Arlo turned towards the entrance of the tent as two legionnaires carried another wounded transgressor into the shelter. They laid him on the ground. A tourniquet was tightly wrapped around his upper arm.

Jake walked up to the transgressor and felt for the neck pulse.

Nothing.

He checked for a femoral pulse.

Still nothing.

Jake asked the legionnaires, "He's dead. Why did you bring him in here?"

"Healer, he was alive on the battlefield. We tied a tourniquet."

Jake shook his head. He inspected the corpse. Checked his head, neck, chest, and abdomen.

Nothing abnormal.

Jake inspected the corpse's legs.

Blood.

He shook his head and said, "He bled out through an artery in his lower right leg. See?"

Jake showed the wound to the two legionnaires and asked, "Don't they teach you to inspect from head to toe in the basic lifesaver course? He'd be alive with a simple tourniquet on his leg."

"Yes Healer Jake, it's...it's just tough out there. Its dark, cold, wet, and three of my friends died today. I haven't slept in over a day."

Jake silently cursed himself.

With empathy he apologized, "I'm sorry. I shouldn't have snapped. It's been a long day for all of us. You tried your best. You lived the Legionnaire Code. After helping your brothers, you provided assistance to your foe."

The two legionnaires held their heads low and departed the tent.

Arlo added, "Such a needless waste of life. What's the stat? Half of all combat deaths are from blood loss to an arm or leg injury?"

Jake answered, "Yeah, it's probably higher. Maybe three out of five combat deaths. A simple inspection and tourniquet is all that's needed."

Arlo replied, "But with that monsoon, our fatigue, and those conditions out there, that statistic is no longer so shocking."

"Arlo, but still, there's nothing more torturous in our line of work than watching men succumb to death that could have been saved from the use of a simple tourniquet."

Jake had to shift his mind and focus on something else.

He glanced around the tent. There must have been over twenty wounded prisoners lying in cots and on the floor. He then noticed two men, not in uniform, standing next to one of the cots. They were speaking to the wounded transgressors.

Strange.

Arlo acknowledged Jake's look of confusion.

Arlo said, "Legists."

Jake's eyebrows cringed.

He asked, "Legists? Why?"

"I don't know. They arrived right before you got here. I haven't had a chance to ask."

Jake replied, "I'll talk to them."

Arlo, more junior in rank, nodded. He dipped his bloodied hands into a bowl of red water. He turned to the messenger. The messenger nodded and understood the non-verbal request for clean water. He walked outside.

Jake approached the two legists.

"Gentlemen, the wounded need rest. Please, if it's not urgent, please return tomorrow."

The two legists shot Jake a cold look.

"It IS urgent."

Jake replied, "If I may ask—"

"No you may not."

Both legists turned back to the wounded prisoners lying on their cots. Jake didn't feel like fighting. He'd lose. The legists weren't in uniform. He had no authority over them. Healers long ago lost the authority to run their own tents—at least in the legion. He wasn't

14

sure if the same applied back home. He wondered if his sister, Jenny, would experience similar rules as a civilian healer.

Jake said to the legists, "If you need anything, we'll be over here."

The men of law didn't acknowledge Jake. They kept talking to the wounded transgressors. Jake couldn't understand all that they were saying. He didn't need to. He figured out why they were here. Jake walked back to Arlo.

Jake asked, "I could use some fresh air. Walk outside?"

"Sure, I could use a shower too. This torrential downpour is something."

Both men stepped into the rain. They walked by the messenger carrying two buckets of fresh water.

Arlo said, "Thank you. Go get some rest."

The messenger nodded.

Jake asked, "What do you think?"

"About the legists? This war?"

Arlo bit his lip after saying "war". He looked around for his boss.

Jake said, "Don't worry, the boss is sleeping. The friar had the same concern."

Arlo warned, "Be careful. If the boss catches the friar, we're in for it. And it's outrageous we can't say the word 'war'. They are kidding themselves."

A frustrated Jake shook his head in agreement and said, "Where do they get these terms? Transgressors!? Man-induced disasters? Mere criminals can't defeat our top legion in battle. You know, we're lucky. If it wasn't for the rain and mud, they would have overrun all of us by now. This isn't the same as the Pancho Incident last year in the Southwest. Remember that?"

Arlo said, "Not really, it was my final year at healer school. Didn't pay much attention to the newspapers."

"A small group of bandits from one of the empires on the southern continent landed on our shores. The local protectors were overwhelmed. By the time the legion arrived, the bandits burned down three towns and killed dozens. It was the first time foreigners attacked our soil since the Great War."

Arlo added, "Ok, it's coming back to me now. The legion basically annihilated them on the battlefield, right? They didn't take many prisoners. Ok, so what?"

"Do you remember what happened to the commander and his ranking legionnaires?"

"Not really."

"Fired. They apparently used too much force on the battlefield. The legion was too effective."

Arlo added, "And now our bosses are afraid of repeating that here in the Southeast with these 'transgressors'?"

"Arlo, those legists were giving them Arturo Rights."

"You're kidding me? The same Arturo Rights that protectors give to thieves and criminals after arresting them?"

"You got it, the right to remain silent. The Presiding Chief took a lot of heat for the Pancho Incident."

"Heat from whom? Those bandits got everything they deserved."

"Healer school must have really locked you up. He got heat from the elite, scholarly experts, and most Enlightened elders. Of course the news magnified it out of proportion."

"I really was stuck in the books. I missed all of that."

Jake shook his head again, "I guess that explains why the Southeast is practically under invasion, why our legion was nearly defeated, and why the only thing our general has done is send two legists into our prisoner tent."

"Jake, I think it's worse than that."

Jake nodded, "I agree. Every wounded legionnaire I spoke with said if it wasn't for the mud we'd all be dead. Mud subdued those 'transgressors'…not the legion."

Arlo's face grew white. Fear streamed into his body. He remembered what multiple prisoners told him earlier in the day. He now fully realized what was happening in the Southeast.

Arlo shivered in the warm rain. He felt nauseous.

Jake asked, "Arlo, what is it?"

"There are more waves of transgressors coming to the Southeast. This attack is only the beginning."

Chapter 3

Avanoor

The commander of the local law enforcement, Head Protector Willard Gallatae, asked, "Any updates on the Southeast?"

"It's under control," the village administrator said.

"That's it? Under control? The original news sounded worse than—"

"Subdued. 'The transgressors have been subdued.' That's what they said."

Willard replied, "Transgressors? The first report made it sound like a barbarian horde landed on our southern shores. I would have thought—"

The village administrator cut him off, "Those reports were inaccurate. Plus, the Continent's strongest legion is there assisting the local law enforcement. I'm not shocked that everything is under control."

A cool breeze welcomed the two men chatting on Avanoor's main street during the humid and sticky summer afternoon. The administrator didn't convince Willard. The head protector's son, Jake, was in that legion.

The administrator pointed a few blocks to the west and asked, "Is that Old John again? That foolish Heartless."

Willard squinted. A gaggle of people surrounded an old man standing atop a barrel.

Willard replied, "Yes, that's him."

The administrator hissed, "The Heartless aren't welcome in Avanoor, especially if they are bold and loud."

"I'm sure it's nothing. The Heartless are all but extinct."

The administrator shook his head, "Extinct?! I must disagree. And it's not my job, but I will have to inform the Federals if he's doing what I think."

Willard attempted to defuse the village administrator, "I wouldn't worry about it. He's harmless."

Federals were career bureaucrats on the central government's payroll. They lived in each town to enforce the laws of the capital—Federal City.

The administrator and the head protector walked within earshot of Old John's words. The two men listened.

"A right is a gift from God that extends from our humanity. Our rights are a natural part of our humanity. We own our bodies, thus we own the gifts that emanate from our bodies. Our right to life. Our right to think as we wish, to say what we think, to publish what we say. Our right to worship or not worship. Our right to travel, to defend ourselves, to use our own property as we see fit. Our right to due process, which is fairness from the Federals, and our right to be left alone are all rights that stem from our humanities. And we, the people, loan the government power to protect these rights."

The village administrator grabbed Willard's arm and said, "I'm serious. No matter how harmless and how old, he shouldn't be saying those words. Look at all those people listening. The last thing the Continent needs are more Heartless."

Willard replied, "He's probably just on a tangent. You know how the people love hearing his war stories and how those parables sometimes drift."

Willard's father served with Old John in the Great War. Old John was nearly an uncle to him. Deep inside, Willard was also a Heartless, but he could never live it. He could never admit it. No one could ever learn that Avanoor's head protector was a Heartless. Willard feared the repercussions on his family and close friends. It'd be the end of his career at the minimum. His family would become social outcasts.

Federals could not legally banish Heartless from towns and cities. However, they had other unofficial methods for silencing, discrediting, humiliating, and even removing Heartless from society.

Old John was considered a sacred citizen due to his hero status from the Great War. His charismatic ability to entrance younger generations with his parables magnified that status. However, the element of veteran sanctity had only slowed the Federals in their drive to marginalize and repudiate him.

The administrator and Willard continued walking towards John. They listened to the old man standing on an oak barrel.

"The Divine gave us these rights at our conception. These are natural rights that we were born with. The Federals don't give them to us, the Federals don't pay for them, and the Federals can't take them away unless a jury finds that we have violated someone else's rights. What is a good?" John asked.

Willard saw the administrator's hands clench as they maneuvered through the crowd to the front.

Willard interrupted, "John, you really need to get off the barrel. If the Federals hear—"

John looked down at Willard.

"Young Willard, how are you doing?"

"John, come on down off the barrel. The Federals are a few blocks away."

Old John replied, "Young Willard. Protector Willard. Let the Federals hear me. Maybe they'll finally understand the Truth. The Truth is coming. The Truth will return."

Willard turned and shot the administrator a look.

Calm down. I got this.

The administrator, his fists fully clenched, hesitantly nodded.

Willard said, "Ok John. If you're not down from the barrel by the time I return, I'm going to have to get the Federals."

Old John nodded and winked. Willard waved at the administrator. The two men walked away from the crowd. They could still hear the old man.

"A good is something that we want or need. Goods are not rights. We have our rights from birth. However, we purchase goods that we require for existence. Shelter is a good. Clothing is a good. A horse is a good."

John paused. He looked at Willard and the administrator walking away.

John turned back to the crowd and said, "And food is a good."

The administrator shook his head and said, "I'm going to have to tell the Federals."

"He'll stop. I'll talk to him tonight. Ok? Give him a break."

He replied, "A break? He's lucky he's still here. He shouldn't be marginalizing rights. Everyone has the right to eat. I'm glad the Enlightened are about to make it law."

"I'm not disagreeing with you but John is an old man with great stories. You know how he sometimes interjects his fables with his old views. He's just stuck in his ways. I'm sure your grandparents were just like him."

Frustration flashed across the administrator's eyes.

He shot back, "No they weren't. They thought everyone should have the right to eat. The right to a home. The right to healers. They weren't cold hearted brutes like Old John. The Federals need to take care of everyone—"

Willard interrupted him, placed his hand on the administrator's shoulder, and pointed at Old John.

Willard said, "See? The crowd is already dispersing. He's harmless. The Federals have more important issues to worry about than an old man stuck in his ways."

Willard carefully walked the fine line of concealing his inner Heartless and protecting Old John. Over the previous years, Willard had covertly shielded his fellow Heartless in Avanoor and successfully hid his true identity from the Federals. It was a laborious balancing act to maintain such graceless harmony.

Of course, they didn't refer to themselves as Heartless. That was the derogatory word for conservative Traditionalists who strongly opposed the policies of the Enlightened and even some moderate Traditionalists. The Heartless stood by the 243 year old constitution written by Servius—the Document. To them, the core principles of the Document were solidified in stone.

The Enlightened and some moderate Traditionalists believed that the Document was obsolete. The central government's chief executive—the Presiding Chief—led the Enlightened party and turned many members of the Traditionalist party into believers that the Document didn't do enough. It had too many checks and balances. The Document made "getting things done" too difficult. The Enlightened argued that Servius—who led the founding fathers of the Continent—intentionally designed the Document to be highly "flexible" and easily rewritten if future generations determined it to be antiquated. They felt that the Continent needed a reformed Document that granted the central government increased power and responsibility so they could more efficiently address the Continent's problems, reduce poverty, and ensure equality.

Protector Willard said to the administrator, "Old John may have views you don't agree with, but we can't forget that he's one of Avanoor's few remaining veterans of the Great War. He lost three brothers in battle. His wife left him while he was a prisoner of war. I'm still in awe of how he escaped from the enemy. And I'm surprised he pulled himself out of depression and alcoholism in the years after he returned home. Cut him a little slack. He sacrificed a lot. He's gone through more pain and overcome more challenges in one year than most people experience in a lifetime."

The administrator replied, "I do respect his service. And his POW escape story is amazing. But, if I hear him saying such words again, the Federals will know. A few Federals here are retiring soon and I might be invited to become a Federal. I won't let some old man get in my way."

Willard nodded, "Thank you. I'll make sure he sticks with just war stories."

Chapter 4

Federal City (FC) – capital of the Continent

Jenny Gallatae stepped up to the polished wood door. She took a deep breath. Nervousness engulfed her stomach. This interview would determine the next five years of her life. She had to relax her mind. She pictured her ever-calm father, Willard.

Dozens of thoughts raced through her head.

How did Dad do it? How does he block out the nervousness? I already miss my parents. I already miss home.

She looked down at the purple cushioned floor. She forced her mind to focus. The grandeur of the lobby wasn't helping.

The secretary behind Jenny said, "Go ahead. Don't be shy. Healer Aaric doesn't bite often."

Jenny turned around and politely smiled at the secretary sitting at her glossy cherry wood desk.

"Thank you."

Jenny turned back to the door. She knocked on the thick oak.

A deep voice on the other side thundered, "Come in!"

Her sweaty and clammy fingers clenched onto the brass handle. She struggled to open the heavy door. It creaked an inch. She gripped the handle with both hands and pulled the door open. She regained her balance and stepped into the room.

A gray haired old man stood over a glass case. He was looking down at a sword.

Healer Aaric asked, "It's a beauty, isn't it?"

Jenny pushed the door closed to the luxurious office. Paintings covered the ornate walls. A candle lit chandelier glistened from the ceiling. Purple silk curtains hung from the sides of the open windows. Her eyes fell onto the polished sword.

He said, "This is a replica of an Old Avanoorean era weapon."

Jenny shyly walked towards the display case and said, "It's magnificent."

Light glinted off of the fine silver blade. The gold handle radiated in the bright sunlight that filtered through the open windows.

Healer Aaric said, "This sword is modeled off of the one used by Servius in the Savage War over 240 years ago."

Something didn't seem right about the sword. She ignored her gut instinct.

Jenny innocently asked, "Is that the one you used in the Great War?"

He bellowed, "Haha, do I look that old? I didn't fight in the Great War. I was…a student during the war."

"Oh, I'm sorry."

"No worries young lady."

Aaric looked up from the display case. His eyes fell onto a slim beautiful twenty-four year old woman. Her olive skin, brown hair, and soft eyes caught him off guard.

"Welcome to FC."

Jenny asked, "FC?"

Aaric chuckled again, "Haha, FC. Federal City. Where have you been living? The grasslands?"

Slightly offended, Jenny looked down and replied, "Yes."

"I'd expect that from you backward types. I never understood how this great nation was founded in such a horrid land—the land of the Heartless. I'm still amazed that many of you greedy Grasslanders purposely turned to subsistence farming to get out of paying taxes."

Jenny bit her tongue.

That's a myth. Some were forced into subsistence farming because there were no jobs.

Aaric said, "Well, Ms Gallatae, you did leave the grasslands to pursue a Federal job. So maybe you're not one of those greedy types. I'd leave the grasslands too. So, tell me. Besides the obvious reasons for leaving your home, why did you want to be a healer?"

Jenny struggled to conceal her disgust.

"I'm here to help the unfortunate. People need healers. The Federals back home recommended this program."

"I always laugh thinking about a Grasslander helping others. Well, I guess it's possible that the land of imbeciles can produce a few good people. How do you like FC so far? You must be overwhelmed by our sophistication."

Jenny forced another smile, "Yes, it's beautiful here. Everyone is so friendly. Everything is so clean, so impressive. Federal City is truly representative of the greatness of the Continent."

She was warned about the pompous attitude of the Federals and especially the elites. Her mother coached her on how to answer such condescending and insulting questions during interviews. She already had an idea of what to expect. She grew up with Federals governing her home town. As a child in school, children of the Federals harassed and ridiculed her and her neighbors.

Aaric asked, "Where in the grasslands are you from?"

She humbly replied, "Avanoor."

"Ahh. An Avanoorean. My family visited Avanoor when I was a child. A history trip. I must say, I'm glad the capital was moved here. Don't you agree?"

Jenny lied, "Yes."

Jenny silently thanked her mother for preparing her for such questions. It wasn't her nature to tolerate insults. She was proud of her home.

Aaric asked, "What is your heritage?"

Jenny lied again, "My ancestors moved to Avanoor after the war with the southern empires over 200 years ago. I have relatives that fought in the final battle that defeated Proditor and the slave armies. How about yourself, sir?"

She was used to Avanoorean jokes and had prepared herself to keep her calm while answering condescending questions. However, she found it especially difficult to lie about her blood. Yet, she could never admit the truth.

Aaric answered, "I'm mixed. I have North East, Southern, and North West ancestry."

24

He paused, obviously disturbed that her heritage was filled with more history and honor.

"Ok. Enough with the small talk. Do you have your file?"

"Yes sir."

"Go sit down and place it on my desk."

Jenny sat in the chair next to Aaric's desk.

He asked, "Would you like a drink?"

"Yes please. Is that a bottle of Sparkling Regal Majesta mead?"

He walked to his office bar and poured the deep yellow mead into a glass.

"Yes, indeed it is. You know your meads."

Jenny lied again and said, "Oh, my father has never had the honor to taste Regal Majesta, but it's his dream to one day have a sip."

"Well, I can't quite imagine a simple Avanoorean ever drinking the finest mead in the world."

He sat down, pushed a glass of water across the desk to her, and opened her file. He sipped his mead. Aaric's healer school certificate hung on the wall above him.

Jenny read the year that he graduated.

One year before the Great War started?

A burning sensation gripped her stomach. Something wasn't right. She also feared that her attempts to enshroud her growing frustration were futile. Healer Aaric had the power to determine where she would spend the next five years of her life as a healer. Jenny clenched her jaws and focused on maintaining an emotionless composure.

Aaric flipped though the file and said, "It is true. You did graduate first in your class at healer school. And are you sure you want to return home for your residency?"

"Yes sir, Avanoor needs healers."

"Hmm. I'll see what I can do, but we don't have any residency openings in Avanoor at this time."

Jenny slipped. Her eyes widened and jaw dropped. Healer Aaric tilted his head in reaction.

She asserted, "Two healers will finish their residency this year and move to another town. Two other healers will retire next year. Avanoor will only have one healer by next planting season!"

Growing irritated, Aaric coldly stated, "Avanoor can only have one healer. We had to make budget cuts recently. We lowered the town's quota. Here's my decision. You will be a healer here in FC for the PC."

"PC?"

"Yes, PC…that's the Presiding Chief. You know who that is, right? He is the executive branch of our government."

Jenny ignored his condescending words.

"But sir, I really want to help those in my home town."

Aaric responded, "I'm a busy man. I coordinate the Continent's entire 'Right to a Healer' program. You're needed here. And my small team is already overwhelmed with placing healers where we need them. We don't have the time to look into it. And honestly, we don't even accept requests. However, I was feeling nice this morning. And I heard that you are one of the top healer graduates across the Continent."

Healer Aaric's eyes scanned Jenny's body. He smiled and paused as if expecting Jenny to thank him. Instead, she blankly stared.

He continued, "Now, go talk to my secretary. She has your paperwork ready. Ok?"

Jenny asked, "So, I was already assigned to FC before I stepped foot in—"

Healer Aaric interrupted, "You all are. You should feel lucky to have met me. Very few healers do. You are excused."

"But the form asked for my preference. I was told I could choose."

Aaric rolled his eyes, "Choose? We do what's best for the Continent. Are you more concerned about yourself and what you want? Or do you want what's best for the common good?"

"Yes, but, can I request a transfer when—"

"No. The decision is final. You're dismissed."

He pushed her file across the table. He stood up and walked to the display case with his mead in hand. His back faced Jenny. She stood and glared at him. The next five years of her life had been pre-determined. A few minutes of effort on their side and they could have assigned Jenny to her home town.

She fought the anger contorting her face. A thick blanket of exasperation wrapped around her head. She froze as she realized she never had any say in her own career.

No say in her own life.

The Federals back home misled her. They told her she could choose.

She lost her breath. The feeling of control over her own life was ripped out of her hands. She shut her eyes. She realized she never had control. Her throat clenched. She wasn't sure what to do. Blood rushed into her head. Half of her wanted to cry. The other half wanted to confront Aaric. However, her instincts knew better.

This happened for a reason.

Her eyes opened. She gained control of her emotions and composure. She grabbed the brass handle to the thick oak door with one hand and swung it open.

Chapter 5

"A man must know his destiny. If he does not recognize it, then he is lost. By this I mean, once, twice, or at the very most, three times, fate will reach out and tap a man on the shoulder. If he has the imagination, he will turn around and fate will point out to him what fork in the road he should take, if he has the guts, he will take it."
– General George S. Patton

The Northern Territory

The magenta morning sun crept above the eastern horizon. Surrounded by a green ocean of prairie grass, a young man sitting on a boulder looked up at a formation of geese flying overhead. Three days of stubble grew on his face. His bloodshot eyes stared back down at the dark western horizon. He scratched the side of his chin under the bulge in his cheek. A small pile of broken sunflower seeds at his feet scattered in a burst of chilly morning air. His faithful dog, Winston, snarled.

"Easy boy."

Fletcher scratched behind the ears of his liver-brown spaniel. He turned back to the east. He watched his sheep munching on the dew covered grass as he walked to his camp. He tossed a few pieces of dried dung in the anemic fire. He stirred the tea leaves in the tin kettle and cracked open a few eggs. They sizzled on the pan.

28

The frigid morning wind of the Northern Territory absorbed the smell of eggs. Fletcher's friend, waking from a full night's sleep, lifted his head off the ground.

Gust scratched his head, yawned, and said, "Ahh, the sound and smell of eggs."

Fletcher replied, "Rise and shine, bro."

Gust yawned again, "Are those wolves still to the west?"

"Yup, and Winston has been itching to go after them again."

"That dog's boldness will get him killed."

Winston tilted his head at Gust.

Gust chuckled, "That's right boy. You heard me."

Fletcher petted his dog's head and said, "And his boldness saved both of us last night."

"I'm with you on that one. First eggs shall go to Winston."

The dog smiled, licked his chops, and wagged his tail.

Fletcher Gallatae had a different calling in life than his younger siblings—Jake and Jenny.

Fletcher came from a long line of protectors and healers. After serving in the legion for five years, he enrolled in Avanoor's protector academy. He originally looked forward to a long career following in his father's footsteps.

However, everything changed when news of the Horse Tax hit Avanoor. Shock rippled through his home town. Anger and then submission followed. No one wanted to give up their horse, but no one could afford the tax.

Their anger eventually faded. What they learned from the experts facilitated their acquiescence.

The harshest drought in decades had parched the Continent's fertile land. Experts, Federals, and scholars claimed the Horse Tax was necessary to save the clouds and stop the drought from turning catastrophic. The Presiding Chief and the Enlightened justified the tax with scientific studies blaming the drought on gases and manure from horses and livestock. They alarmed the nation that an economic depression would be imminent if they did nothing. They only gave the citizens of the Continent two months to sell their horses.

After a couple weeks, like everyone else, Fletcher's anger subsided. He researched every possible way to keep his horse. He crunched the numbers. The tax was unaffordable. He scrutinized the law for any exemptions for protectors or veterans. There were none. Even his father, Willard, the Head Protector of Avanoor was not exempt from the tax. Only a handful of the highest ranking Federals in Avanoor would be exempt.

That's when the sleepless nights hammered him. Fletcher began doubting his childhood dream to serve as a protector. With the little sleep he did experience, he dreamt of riding. He dreamt of galloping through the endless grasslands. In the dreams, snow was falling in the Great Rolling Hills. He rode with the wind at his back.

Something was pulling him.

A magnet. Some indefinable force.

He didn't understand it, but he had to keep his horse. He had to leave Avanoor and move out of the jurisdiction of the Continent.

He replayed the dream during the day. Each night, it consumed him as he floated in an agonizing state of half-consciousness. Mentioning the persistent dream and thoughts of leaving Avanoor only invited strange looks and comments.

Fletcher's family and friends logically debated that a horse wasn't worth sacrificing a career as a protector. They warned him that fleeing the Continent just to keep his horse was absurd. Logic was on the side of his parents and friends. All conversations concluded that the smartest and safest decision was to remain a protector and that he should do what everyone else was doing—give up the horse.

Since permanent residents of FC were exempt from the tax, Fletcher's family and friends were selling their horses to businessmen from FC. Gaining permanent residency there was as infeasible as affording the tax.

Fletcher's persistent dreams only bolstered his resolve to keep his horse. Constructive dialogue with his parents, friends, and fellow protectors quickly transformed into heated debates and arguments.

However, Fletcher knew it wasn't about the horse. Originally it was, but after a month of soul searching he discovered it was something else. It wasn't some stubborn desire to beat the system. It wasn't an urge to make a statement. It was more than that. He could feel it, but not describe it. He could see it, but not say it. He tried explaining it to friends and family. They replied with more blank stares and strange looks. Whatever it was, it was right. It felt right. He had to keep his horse.

Near the end of the two months, days away from the deadline for selling his horse, Fletcher crossed paths with Old John.

Even though most Avanooreans wrote the old man off as a crazy entertaining story teller, Fletcher had different feelings. Old John was best friends with his grandfather. Fletcher never met his grandfather. Old John's adventures made for endless stories during Fletcher's childhood. The parables were so colorful Fletcher easily imagined himself riding with his young grandfather across the Continent, getting into trouble, chasing girls, and fighting in the Great War. Sometimes he felt as if his grandfather was speaking to him through Old John.

Fletcher clearly remembered talking to Old John days before the Horse Tax deadline. They discussed the tax and Fletcher's dilemma. Fletcher didn't even tell Old John about the dreams. He felt that he didn't have to. It was as if Old John could read Fletcher's soul—see inside his heart.

That brief chat with Old John burned into his memory. He could never forget Old John's words.

It is by design that ambiguity cloaks the true path of one's life. You must open your eyes to the light of your heart; it is through this the Divine speaks. And when this path leads you into the inevitable bog of despondency, steer clear of respite. Be not tempted by comfort. Rather, focus on the light. Stay on the path. Do not slow, do not waiver. For you will soon discover what He has planned.

Fletcher made his decision after speaking with Old John. The son of Willard slept peacefully that night for the first time in two months.

His family and friends were disappointed but respected it. Few tried to talk him out of the decision. Within two days, he was riding north.

Fletcher placed three eggs on a slice of oat bread. He shook his pepper container over the eggs and spooned some honey onto them.

He held out Winston's favorite breakfast and said, "Here boy."

Winston ignored the food and jumped on all four paws. He focused his attention to the west. He growled. Both Fletcher and

31

Gust stared in amazement at the dog turning his head from the breakfast.

The flock of sheep grabbed the two men's attention. The animals stopped grazing and froze. Three lambs scurried into the middle of the flock. The two men turned their eyes back to Winston as he sprang over the fire and sprinted west.

Fletcher gripped the scabbard of his sword. Gust reached for his bow and arrows. They looked past their long morning shadows.

Five wolves raced towards their camp. Winston galloped straight at them.

Chapter 6

Federal City

Jenny leapt over a puddle on the maroon brick sidewalk. Between the stone road and sidewalk, damp grass and knee high bushes shimmered in the sunlight. The morning rain clouds had opened to a clear blue sky. A four-wheeled carriage on the road pulled by a horse splashed water over the bushes and onto Jenny's legs and open toe leather sandals. Water dripped off her wet ankles. She stopped and watched the carriage pass her. The driver ignored her. She even thought that he purposely swerved near the curb to hit the puddle.

Jenny's Grasslander clothing and fashion invited unfriendly attention. She kept reminding herself to shop for some more appropriate clothes after her first paycheck. She was already tired of the dirty looks, quiet comments, and general rudeness of people after only one week living in FC.

FC locals held their noses up to Avanooreans and people from the Great Rolling Hills. She definitely needed to stop wearing leather sandals and her leather belt. Those were the first things FC locals noticed. Her long brown hair, olive skin, and her clothes were the next obvious.

"Jenny!"

She looked across the road through the heavy traffic of horse pulled carriages. Jenny smiled. It was Chloe. Jenny waved as her roommate crossed the street dodging the horse traffic.

33

"Chloe! So great to see you! Are you heading back home?"

Chloe hunched forward with rings under her eyes and nodded her head.

She replied, "Long night and I'm starving."

Jenny asked, "Are they still—"

"Yeah, they are incredible. I don't even pay attention, but it must be important. All night again."

"Is this normal? It's my first week and it's tough to think that this is routine."

Chloe answered, "No, this is strange. It's been actually a lax residency until recently."

"Is it due to the war?"

Chloe placed her hand on Jenny's shoulder, looked around, and said, "Shhh, don't say that word. We're not at…you know. It's being subdued."

Jenny moved into Chloe's two-story, three bedroom brick home a few days earlier. A fellow Grasslander healer who has lived in FC for a couple years, Chloe took Jenny under her wing.

Chloe asked, "Your brother is down there, right?"

"Yup, I need to send Jake our address. He writes home regularly. He probably doesn't know I'm here yet."

"Oh, I hope he's fine."

"I'm sure he is. Trouble always finds him, but he always manages to find his way out."

Chloe said, "Ha, my older brother was like that. He just got married though. Finally settling. Hey, do you have time for a tea?"

Jenny answered, "Yeah, I'm actually a little early. I kept waking up from nervousness. I was afraid of sleeping in."

"Ha, I had the 'new gal nervous syndrome' too. Well, there's a neat looking tea shop that just opened a block from here past Licensing Row."

Jenny asked, "Licensing Row?"

"Yeah, it's were you go to get your license."

"What kind of license?"

"Professional licenses."

Jenny asked, "Like a legist license? Healer license?"

"Kinda, but for lower level jobs. A friend of mine just earned his Pall Bearer License. All the road safety coordinators, street cleaners, and landscapers need to go there for their licenses. There's probably dozens of licenses and each have their own uniform and—"

Jenny interrupted, "Pall Bearer License?"

Chloe rolled her eyes, "I keep forgetting you've been stuck in the grasslands. Have you heard of the phrase 'Health and Safety'?"

"Well, yeah, but I don't know the story behind it."

Chloe said, "Ok, let's get some tea first then I'll explain it to you."

The two young healers walked down the main street of Federal City. The city amazed Jenny. The average building in FC was the same height as the tallest buildings back home. Everyone owned horses. The luxurious carriages enthralled her. Homes were twice the size of those in Avanoor. Lush green trees and trimmed bushes lined the streets. Everything was clean and new looking. Even the side streets were cleaner than Avanoor's main street. Jenny has never seen so much effort put into landscaping grass, bushes, and trees. FC was truly a bustling and beautiful city.

Jenny asked, "Quick question, how hard was it to buy your home?"

"Easy, why? Are you thinking of buying?"

"Not right now, but maybe in a year or two."

"That's what I did…waited about a year to buy. But it was easy. The government encourages banks to lend money to anyone who asks for it. That's how I got a loan that required no money down. Oh, here it is, we nearly walked past it."

They turned off the sidewalk and into the tea shop.

A young female barista said, "Good morning! Welcome to Fragrance Teas. Would you like to try our grand opening special?"

The barista smiled at Chloe and Jenny. The two women didn't respond to the young girl. The barista understood why. Most of the customers reacted the same way. The extensive and flashy menu hanging on the wall entranced the two healers.

Chloe asked Jenny, "What are you having? Tea on me."

Jenny continued staring at the menu, "Umm."

Chloe smiled, "Overwhelming, eh? No worries, you'll be fluent in FC's sophistication soon."

Jenny ignored Chloe's remark and said, "I need another five minutes just to read that thing."

The barista added, "And there's more than just what's up there. You can customize and—"

Jenny surrendered, "Chloe, you know what, I'll just have whatever you order."

The barista smiled after taking Chloe's order. The two women walked to the side of the tea shop while their teas were brewed.

Jenny asked, "So, 'Health and Safety' and pallbearers?"

"Oh yeah, right. After FC granted all citizens the Right to a Healer a decade ago, they began a 'Health and Safety' campaign. The best way to stay healthy and not need a healer was to live healthy and safely. If FC could make our lives healthier and safer, it would save money on healer expenses."

Jenny added, "Yeah, I remember now."

"People need the Federals to keep them safe and healthy. Many people are unfortunate and need help…especially the children. If it wasn't for the ingenious legislation generated on Elder Hill and the PC's magical signature, the world would be such a darker place. But I digress. So, originally, FC accidentally stumbled into the 'Health and Safety' campaign. Before the Horse Tax, horse accidents were a leading cause of death. After the tax was approved, many people stopped owning horses. Obviously, fewer horses resulted in fewer accidents. Thousands of lives were saved each year. Since then, FC has done a great job at instituting many laws and regulations to keep everyone safer. That's where the Pallbearer License, Traffic Safety License, Garbage Removal License and basically all of License Row came from. Rules are coming out every month banning unhealthy foods and—"

Jenny chuckled, "But seriously, Pallbearer License? Landscaping License? What's the risk in that?"

"You may laugh…but a lot of people are injured every year when they trip on steps while carrying heavy coffins. You'd be shocked at how dangerous planting and pruning trees can be. And many of these regulations actually create jobs! The pallbearer profession didn't exist until the law was made. It's all perfect! Jobs are saved or created. We citizens are safer and healthier. With a happy, healthy, and employed population, we make fewer visits to the healer and save the Federals money! Saved money can be spent on even more programs to make the Continent even better. It's really magical how ingenious the Enlightened—"

The barista yelled, "Order for Chloe!"

The two women turned to the counter, picked up their teas, and walked outside. They sat at a wood table under the partial shade of a tree.

Jenny knew her history. None of what Chloe said actually worked. Federal City was wealthy and booming because it sucked the wealth from the rest of the Continent.

"So Chloe, I've barely seen you these past few days. We need to have some girl time. And I need some local fashion advice."

"I know, you're soooo Grasslander. You'll be one of us in no time. I can't believe that I lived like a Grasslander just a couple years ago."

Jenny bit her tongue and said, "Yes, I…ahhh…look forward to fitting in."

"So, our alternating schedules have been keeping us from really chatting. How do you like the residency so far?"

Jenny replied with her rehearsed answer, "I'm honored to have been chosen to work in the Presiding Chief's office."

Chloe's eyes lit up. Jenny was glad Chloe didn't see through the forced smile and not-so-true answer.

"You're right about that! They only pick the best and the brightest to work in FC and the best of the best to work on Elder Hill and with the PC. Wonderful man, isn't he?"

"Yes, but I've only met him once briefly."

"Oh, you'll have more time with him. Remember, you're his personal healer…well, apprentice healer."

"Chloe, I actually have a question about that. When does the Presiding Chief's official healer return? I've been praying nothing serious happens while he's out. It's been overwhelming…this incredible responsibility during the first week of my residency. How do you do it?"

Chloe sipped her tea and replied, "Well, first, everyone calls the Presiding Chief 'PC'. People will look at you funny when you spell out 'Presiding Chief'. But yeah, the PC's main healer rarely takes trips like these. I think he returns next week. Don't sweat it. I'll introduce you to other experienced healers working on Elder Hill that can help in case of an emergency. They are only minutes away."

"Thank you. I really appreciate all of your help. I'd be lost without you."

Chloe's smile radiated. Her pearly white teeth glistened. Jenny thought Chloe looked similar to herself.

Tall, slender, beautiful curves.

Chloe's dark brown hair and olive skin caught many looks. Her deep blue eyes sparkled.

One exception—Chloe had amazing FC fashion sense. Jenny looked forward to experiencing FC nightlife and shopping. She's heard a lot about the bars and the large crowd of young educated professionals, like herself, living in FC.

Chloe said, "It's my pleasure. I'm happy to take care of a fellow Grasslander. Adjusting here wasn't fun. But after a few months you'll be one of us and you'll have the time of your life."

Jenny forced another smile. She wasn't sure about that. She was still sore at Healer Aaric's decision.

Jenny asked, "So, do you know why everyone on Elder Hill is staying up late?"

"I think it's about the Right to Eat. Not too sure really. I don't pay much attention. I've heard that phrase thrown around a lot. Don't worry about what they do. They are genius people with teams of experts advising them on such high-level policies. We're just healers. Oh, and I should probably tell you…when you're not healing, you're serving tea to the PC and his staff."

"Haha, I've already noticed that. I've served more tea in the last few days than I've consumed in the last year. I'm looking forward to healer work though. I've always wanted to be one."

Chloe placed her empty tea cup on the table, "I was like you…dreamt of using what I learned at healer school to help others. And you will get the opportunity. They'll send us off for a month each year on short missions. I went on a diplomatic trip with the PC to Anic last year and helped out some impoverished sick children."

"Anic?"

"It's one of the more powerful empires on the southern continent. But, yeah, start learning your teas and I'll introduce you to FC…and the many malls, bars, and shoe stores within walking distance of our home."

Jenny smiled, "I look forward to it."

Chloe asked, "Why do you think I volunteered for the night shift?"

"Shopping?"

Chloe smiled, "Well, I should probably get back home. My bed is calling my name."

Jenny chuckled, "And I need to get going too. The PC is probably looking for his tea girl."

"Quick learner! You'll love it here."

The two healers parted ways. Jenny waved bye. She turned around and looked down the road towards Elder Hill. She watched a man in a red uniform shoveling poop off the street. Behind him, a woman wearing a green uniform directed horse carriage traffic. Jenny looked to her right. A man wearing a yellow uniform clipped the tops of bushes next to the sidewalk.

Chapter 7

The Southeast

The General said, "Men, I am pleased to announce that the transgressors have been subdued. We will leave this wretched swampland tomorrow. We'll make camp on the hill a half-day to the north and let the earth dry before we return south to apprehend the remaining transgressors."

Jake stood in the back of the conference tent listening to the old man speak. Underneath the thinned gray hair were sharp wrinkles, a cherry red face, and beady eyes. His crisp uniform was decorated with a chest full of medals and ribbons. He needed a stepping block at the podium to make up for his short stature.

Jake leaned over and whispered into Arlo's ear, "How does he wear that thick stuffy uniform in this heat?"

Arlo whispered back, "I think he's insane. And where did he get all of those medals? He's got more than my grandfather did from the Great War…and the General was just a child at the time."

Someone turned around and glared at the two healers.

"Shh."

The hot and stuffy tent was packed with senior legionnaires and legists.

The General continued, "You men have fought bravely and sacrificed much to assist the local protectors return order to our shores."

Jake couldn't believe what he was hearing.

"Tell your men that you all will be decorated and receive a months of rest and relaxation after our mission is complete. And I want to inform you that we are following the strict legal code set forth by our astute legists. Each transgressor has been given Arturo Rights and will face a fair trial. We must show the world that our justice system is strong."

While speaking, the General stood awkwardly and nervously playing with his fingers. He stepped off the wood box and began pacing. The General tried to speak with confidence and directness, but Jake could hear the uncertainty in his voice. Jake could see that the General knew the transgressors were far from being subdued. The General knew that these transgressors nearly wiped out his legion. The "wretched swampland" saved them.

Jake ducked out the back slit in the tent. Arlo curiously followed.

"What are you doing?"

Jake replied, "I can't listen to that guy. He's going to get us all killed."

Jake froze. His eyes fell on the General's traveling tent.

He said, "Arlo, look at that."

"Well, yeah, they are packing his tent. So? The General said we're moving to the north to dry ground."

"No, no. Not his main tent. Look further to the right. You see the aide?"

Jake pointed to the General's aide preparing the smaller tent for travel.

Arlo said, "No way."

Jake added, "Why would they unpack the traveling tent if we're just moving to the hill a few hours north?"

"What? Do you think he's heading all the way back to FC?"

Jake replied, "Where else?"

Arlo said, "The General must know about the second and third waves of transgressors."

Jake said, "He didn't pick that hill for dry ground. He picked that because a hill is the best place to set up a defense."

Arlo added, "A defense when he just told us we're going on the offense after the ground dries. My God. He's leaving us to fend for ourselves."

"And he's fleeing to save his own hide. Coward."

The head healer walked out of the General's tent.

Arlo said, "Let's go ask the boss about it."

Jake hesitated, "Ah...let me do it."

Jake approached the boss.

"Healer Jake, how is everyone?"

"We lost one yesterday to gangrene. The others are getting stronger."

"Good, good. Hey, I have some news for you."

Jake gulped. He knew what was coming.

His boss continued, "You should be proud. You did a fine job. The Continent is happy for your service. Jake, you heard what the General said, right?"

"Yes."

His boss looked down.

"Jake. The General won't be staying with the legion after we head north. He's returning to Federal City. I'm going with him. You, Arlo, and the other healers will remain with the wounded and the legion. You'll be needed here."

Jake forced himself to look shocked as if he didn't already know.

"Sir, the wounded need to return with you. This is no place for them to remain. Better care is—"

"I know, I know. However, the wounded will slow the General. He's needed back in FC ASAP. Plus, the General needs one healer with him at all times. That'll be me. We're not taking the wounded."

"Sir, respectfully. That's bull. We're outnumbered. There is no way, no matter how well the legion is dug in, that we'll defend that hill and protect the wounded. You need to take the wounded with—"

"Careful young Lieutenant. Stay in your lane."

"Sir, we need another legion just to halt the transgressor's advance. If the wounded stay, they are as good as dead...along with the legion."

"Jake—"

"Sir, we are talking about thousands of legionnaires that will either be dead or captured after that land dries."

"Jake, you're no more than twenty-five years old. You're young, inexperienced, and don't understand all of the dynamics. The General wears stars on his uniform for a reason. He's privy to information that you don't have. Now, I have to pack. You're lucky

I'm reasonable. I could have placed you on report for your insubordinate behavior."

Jake firmly said, "Insubordination? Slapping you with reality is insubordination? Doing the right thing is insubordination?"

Aghast, the vertically challenged Major opened his mouth unable to find any words.

Jake scowled down at the stumpy Major, "All you care about is your career. The blood of my comrades is nothing to you. What happened to the legion's Healer Code? 'Never leave your patients. Never desert those who sacrificed in battle. Protect them at all costs.' Sir, you are a shame. No, you are a disgrace."

The Major's face glowed red hot. He knew the young healer was correct. The boss was running from almost certain death and pulled rank to save his own hide. He knew that he spat on the code that all legionnaire healers swore to. But Jake crossed the line.

The Major's lip curled. He gripped Jake's collar with one hand, jerked the young healer's head down, and hissed into his ear.

"And if you survive the transgressors I WILL end your career. I will strip your commission and dishonorably discharge you from the legion for cowardice. I'll make sure the remainder of your life is spent in the craphole of society. It's a long ride back to FC and I'll be sitting next to the General the entire way. You might as well consider yourself an outcast effective immediately."

Evil flashed across the Major's eyes. Jake didn't flinch. He stood firm and smirked at his gutless boss.

The Major released Jake's collar, turned, and briskly waddled away.

Arlo ran up to Jake and said, "Did you just do that?"

"Arlo, get to the healer tents. All wounded that can ride horses and survive the trip to FC leave tonight. The others...we'll do what we can for them here."

"But Jake, what about us? The legion?"

"The wounded that can travel must go first. We will stay. The legion will need us."

Arlo stuttered, "But...but—"

Jake grabbed both of Arlo's shoulders and said, "Arlo, our nation is under attack. My family is three weeks away in Avanoor. Your family is five weeks away. The transgressors have tens of thousands more warriors headed to our shores right now. Thousands are waiting on the other side of that mud waiting to attack the moment the land dries. We are all that stands between the invaders and our loved ones."

Chapter 8

The Northern Territory – New Avanoor

Winston woke to find himself strapped onto Fletcher's horse. Sharp pain shot through his right shoulder and left hind leg. He winced as they entered New Avanoor.

Fletcher, walking alongside the horse, noticed his buddy was awake and panting.

"Almost home boy, almost home."

Five years earlier Fletcher arrived in the Northern Territory and built an earthen home next to a creek. His fifteen sheep grazed the sweet grasses and drank the cold water. However, Fletcher wasn't the only citizen of the Continent to migrate north to keep his horse.

What was once a barren stretch of prairie, with only one pioneer and his faithful dog, transformed into a fast growing bustling town. Thousands of migrants flowed north each summer—the Great Migration. Other settlements sprang up throughout the Northern Territory. Abundant land, lush grasses, and the freedom to own horses and livestock drew many impoverished Grasslanders to the Northern Territory and out of the choking jurisdiction of FC. The brutal winters no longer deterred migrants looking for a new start. A society of people, filled with the pioneer spirit, burgeoned in the north. Fletcher's settlement quickly grew into the largest town in the Northern Territory. It became known as New Avanoor.

Fletcher patted his dog and loosened one of the bandages. The bleeding had stopped, but he needed to clean the wounds.

"You're lucky to be alive boy."

Winston barked.

"Don't worry. Gust is watching over the sheep."

Fletcher looked around. New Avanoor seemed to change every time he returned from his flock. Earthen homes, stables, and shops seemed to pop up overnight. Fletcher thought to himself how a little freedom, even in the most barren of places, fueled such growth and prosperity.

"Fletcher! What happened?"

Protector Kinton, on his horse, trotted to Fletcher.

"Winston took on a pack of wolves and killed two by the time Gust and I arrived. We finished off the others."

Kinton dismounted his horse and patted Winston, "Amazing dog."

Fletcher asked, "Is that one creator still in town?"

"Which one? We've had an influx of them from FC all summer."

"The creator with the messy white hair. He arrived right after the spring melt."

"Yup, he's here. Do you think Winston is infected?"

"I'd rather be safe."

Kinton asked, "Have you visited Creator Precinct yet? I can take you there."

"It's been a busy summer…haven't made it over there yet. Let's drop Winston off at my place first."

The two men and Winston arrived at Fletcher's home. They laid the wounded dog on his bed and headed to the other side of town— Creator Precinct.

On their way Fletcher pointed to a narrow round brick chimney taller than most buildings. It was spewing dark smoke.

"Kinton, what's that?"

The protector replied, "Remember that black rock we found last summer? Well, the hills to the north are full of it. And it burns…burns so good we won't need dried cow dung anymore.

There's so much of it too. The problem is getting it to New Avanoor. The stuff isn't light. But to answer your question, that chimney burns the black rock for experiments."

"Speaking of black rock, how's that new weapon coming along? The one that uses the black powder?"

Kinton chuckled, "Fletcher, you really haven't paid any attention to what's been going on, have you? You should have hired—"

"I know, I know. You were right…I should have hired some help. Our flocks are getting too large for two men to handle."

"Well, get this. You won't need that bow and arrow anymore."

Fletcher's jaw dropped and asked, "They did it?"

"Yup, they said it was simple."

"Stop with the suspense."

Kinton chuckled, "Haha, I'll let the creator tell you. I'll introduce you to her sometime."

The two men dismounted their horses and walked to the door of a brand new earthen home. Kinton knocked. A thin scraggly old man appeared. His long white frizzy hair dangled down to his shoulders. A thick ivory white beard concealed his cheeks and jaw. He held a small spectacle between his eye and a parchment. He looked up at the two men, then back down at the parchment.

He squinted while reading and asked, "Protector Kinton and Chief Fletcher. What may I do for you two fine gentleman on this lovely morning?"

The old creator continued squinting at the parchment. He didn't even look up at the two men.

Fletcher stated, "Winston was wounded by wolves. I'm fearful of—"

He looked up from the parchment and placed his spectacle in his chest pocket and said, "Infection. Yes, yes."

Fletcher asked, "Can you take a look at him?"

"My stalwart young man, of course I will. Give me a moment to retrieve my potion."

The old man drifted behind the door.

Fletcher said, "He's the one I told you about, the creator who traveled up here during this brutal spring."

Kinton replied, "Oh, we talked. Well, more like he vented to me. Science is rotting in FC. Creators, innovators, and even some scholars are fleeing in droves."

"Serious? There's so much money down there. I find it hard to believe—"

"Fletcher, the Federals are allocating all the grant money to study the climate and saving obscure life forms. Remember the story about the fish? How they shut down irrigation to an entire region because it threatened a minnow?"

The door opened and the creator walked outside holding a jar of white paste.

"Gentlemen, take me to your valiant creature."

The men headed towards Fletcher's home.

Fletcher asked, "Creator, can you tell me more about these grants to study the climate?"

"Blobberdash! Those nefarious elite have their heads so high in the clouds they can't see if the laces on their boots need to be tied. They have lost real science. They have forsaken innovation. It's all hubris. Hubris and vanity. Thank God for you Chief Fletcher. Thank God this land has a shining light."

Fletcher was taken aback. Many have complimented him for founding New Avanoor, but never on that scale.

The creator continued, "They demanded that I study 'how is what I'm doing affecting the clouds' or else they would cut my funding. I study mold. The small green fluff that grows on rocks and tree stumps. Do you know why they demanded that I 're-tool' my laboratory?"

"No", both Fletcher and Kinton said.

"Those nittywit miscreants savor power. Do not be fooled into believing that the money they spend and each page of legislation written is for the climate. Ney, all is done for their fancy banquets."

"Huh?" Kinton asked.

"Those parties and frequent banquets on Elder Hill are nothing more than bragging competitions. The first and only banquet I attended ripped me out of the laboratory and opened my eyes to the true intent of the Enlightened. Ask, you may, what drives the Enlightened? It is bragging. Indulging, boasting to each other, and basking in egotistical grandeur. Luxuriating in their power and control over people, money, and decisions. Power over people. They tell the people what to think so that the Enlightened can get their way. That is it. What occurs at those banquets drives the Enlightened."

Fletcher chuckled, "Ha, I'm not too surprised that the elite in FC enjoy flaunting their efforts in 'progressing' society towards 'Utopia'."

The creator interjected, "My wise young friend. Exactly correct, you are. You summarize, in one sentence, my verbose paragraph. God did not bless me with a laconic tongue. But during that banquet, I felt like I stumbled into a putrid abyss of nausea as I listened to elders, both Enlightened and Traditionalist, crow about how many pages of climate saving research they wrote and how many projects they funded. Or how many rodents, bugs, and other pests they protected from us humans. The creators who took the grant money are no better than those elites. The authentic creators and explorers of real science fled FC. After that banquet, I surrendered. I did not accept the grant money and retired from science to live out my remaining years sweeping FC's streets. And then the beetles came. The ground beetles were eating the walls out of my home in FC. I couldn't find an exterminator. You know why?"

Amused, Fletcher shook his head as the three men turned a corner.

The creator continued, "Those elites passed laws to protect 'innocent and endangered life forms'. Protecting a rare bird is fine. But home eating insects? Exterminators don't exist anymore…not for the average citizen. The elite, of course, are granted waivers when their homes are invaded by pests. None of their own rules apply to them…just like the Horse Tax exemption for Federal City."

Kinton added, "Fletcher, being the chief of New Avanoor, I strongly recommend spending more time plugged in here and less time with your sheep. New Avanoor needs their leader."

Fletcher replied, "Well, finding my successor is something we need to talk—"

Kinton cut him off, "Fletcher, the people want you to be the chief…you don't realize the extent of what you've done here. The Northern Territory is booming. New Avanoor is the center for innovation and creation. Just look at what surrounds us. The people need you."

The little town's transformation into a prospering city hadn't sunk in yet. Fletcher's focus was Winston.

Kinton stopped pushing Fletcher. The chief's stubbornness always succeeded in changing the subject. Silence accompanied the men on the remainder of the walk.

They arrived at Fletcher's home and entered.

The creator kneeled and petted Winston.

He said, "My strong creature of God. Wounded while protecting the vulnerable from evil. Nothing more honorable."

Those words sounded familiar to Fletcher. It reminded him of Old John.

The creator looked directly at Fletcher and said, "All that is necessary for evil to triumph is for the good to do nothing."

Fletcher and Kinton looked at each other.

Strange old man.

But those words hit a nerve inside Fletcher. He didn't know why. He didn't know what was upon him.

The creator kneeled down to Winston, applied the potion, and said, "This will protect you from infection…my personal recipe."

The creator winked at Winston.

Chapter 9

The Southeast

Three days of clear blue skies and intense southern sun cooked the earth dry. The army of transgressors had formed at the bottom of the hill outside of the range of the legion's archers. They arrived the night before and did not attack. Confusion and uncertainty proliferated like malignant cancer through the legion. The General was long gone leaving a member of his staff as the acting commander.

Jake entered the Commander's tent and asked, "Sir, I was told you wanted to see me?"

"Yes, yes. Sit down."

"Yes sir."

Jake sat on a wood stool.

"Healer Jake, how are the remaining wounded?"

"Good sir, some are ready to travel north on horses."

"How about the wounded transgressors you and Healer Arlo were tending to?"

"They are improving too, sir."

The Commander mumbled. An air of nervousness encompassed the unsure man. He mumbled again.

Jake asked, "Sir, I couldn't understand—"

"I must ask you to find six of the healthiest prisoners. You will escort them to their army."

Jake forced himself to remain calm.

"I don't...don't understand. Just to confirm, sir, you want me to escort six of their wounded down the hill and into the enemy's camp?"

"Yes."

"May I ask why, sir?"

"Goodwill. Maybe they'll negotiate with me if I return six of their wounded."

"Sir, if I may be candid, you are sending me to my death."

"No...no. You will act as my messenger carrying the Flag of Truce. They will respect international law. If they harm you, that's a direct violation and subject to penalty."

Jake squeezed his eyes shut.

If the transgressors don't kill me, the Major will end my career upon returning home. I have nothing to lose and I'm not going to let a staff officer send me towards certain death.

Jake's lip curled, "Subject to penalty!? Are you going to send a team of legists to issue Arturo Rights and schedule a day in court for violating the Flag of Truce? Or are you planning to use the legion, who is outnumbered three to one, to enforce that law?"

The Commander remained sitting. He didn't react to the young healer's disrespectful tone and insubordinate behavior. Both of them knew that the correct answer to any order, especially the Commander's, was a simple, "Yes, sir."

"Healer Jake, umm...you are right about us being outnumbered. Even though we're dug in defensively on this hill, we'll still lose in battle. But the Flag of Truce, it's the law. They must follow it. And if this buys us goodwill, then their commander and I can meet and work out fair terms for surrender."

Jake said, "FC is only weeks away. My home isn't much further. We are the only legion on this side of the Continent. Even if you meet with the enemy and he doesn't kill you...you can't surrender."

The Commander remained calm and stated, "What parallel universe do we live in when a junior officer is telling a legion commander that he can't do something?"

That caught Jake off guard. This Commander wasn't the usual type of insecure staff officer who would have verbally ripped off Jake's head and then thrown him in the brig for calling out their ineptitude.

Jake didn't reply.

"Healer Jake, everything you say is true, but we must hope they will follow the laws of war. If we fight, then we all die. Surrender is our only option."

Jake calmed himself. This Commander was willing to hold a conversation rather than bark out reckless orders.

The Commander paused and looked at the ground.

He said, "I'm not a career legionnaire. I'm not even a true legionnaire. Are you familiar with my family?"

Confused, Jake shook his head.

Is this guy insane?

"No sir. I don't know of your family. I actually didn't know who you were until the General left a few days back and placed you in charge."

"Healer Jake, I'm in over my head. And yes, I'm confiding in you. None of my advisors had the feedback that you just gave me. They all recommended I use the Flag of Truce, buy goodwill, and negotiate. Foolish sycophants. And I may have never commanded a unit in my career, but I know a wise person when I see one. I know who is worth listening to and when to listen. Rank and age aren't as important as character and common sense."

"Ahh, sir. I don't—"

"My father is a Traditionalist elder in FC. He's had plans for me since I was young. I attended private schools, graduated from the most elite university in FC, and attended legist school. After all that he required I serve in the legion for a few years. He's prepping me to enter FC politics. His father did the same for him. That's why I asked if you knew of my family."

Jake asked, "Ahh, sir, what does this have to do with the army of transgressors that's about to attack us?"

"Let me explain. The General left me behind to 'arrest the remaining transgressors after the earth dried'. And I probably have no more time in the legion than you do."

Jake didn't know what to say. He blankly stared at the son of a Traditionalist elder.

The Commander continued, "The General set a political trap. He put me in charge of a 'simple cleanup' mission. However, it will fail. Who will be the fall guy?"

"Ahhh. You."

"Healer Jake, there's more to it than just that. His family and our family are...umm—"

"Competing?"

"You could say that. It was a perfect scenario for the General. He saves his hide while bringing shame to my family after I fail the 'simple cleanup' mission. The disgrace will be even worse when FC is under threat of foreign invaders. My name, my family's name, will be dragged through the mud as the ones who allowed the capital of the Continent to be under siege for the first time since the southern empires attacked Avanoor over 200 years ago. The upcoming election will be a disaster."

Jake exclaimed, "Commander, there's an army that will defeat us in battle, waves of more armies will arrive soon, FC will surely fall, and all you're concerned about is your family name and the upcoming elections!?"

The Commander calmly replied, "Healer Jake...can I just call you Jake?"

"Ahh, you're the Commander, sir."

"Jake, you are correct. I do sound awfully out-of-touch with reality. But you're probably not too savvy on the politics of FC. War is nothing but the continuation of politics by other means. The point is...the PC will not send more legions. When FC is under direct threat, he'll point his finger at my family and the Traditionalists. And then he'll meet with the transgressors and use his charisma to end the invasion. He is the connoisseur of empty promises. He'll reap the credit for saving FC...and then he'll be re-elected. The PC is one shrewd guy. Trust me, this is complex. I don't want to get too much into the details."

Jake's appalled reaction didn't faze the Commander.

The Commander continued, "But I'll give you a little background. Two main families lead the two political parties of FC—the Traditionalists and the Enlightened. My family leads the Traditionalists and the last decade has been disastrous."

Still disgusted, Jake replied, "You Traditionalists failed to stop the PC's Horse and Livestock Tax, Right to a Healer, and all their other programs. Come on, Save the Clouds? How did they beat you on that one? And half the Traditionalists are no better than the Enlightened—Traditionalists in name only. They compromised their principles to be 'moderate' and 'bipartisan'. You also divorced yourself from the Heartless to appease the Enlightened. They were your base. They represented your principles. You guys deserved to lose power."

"That's all a long story involving closed-door deals, earmarks, buyouts, and strong arm politics. Yes, some Traditionalists sold out their principles and shunned the Heartless. The people of the Continent want politicians to get things done on Elder Hill. The people want compromise, not ideologically driven stalemates. Voters don't like the party of 'No'. So, some Traditionalist elders, as you put it, 'compromised' to get things done. And other Traditionalists compromised as long as their districts benefitted. Did you ever wonder why more healers live in the Northwest? Or why taxes on horses in the Northeast are affordable...to some? Those Traditionalists 'traded' their votes in return for special benefits. The elders voted against their principles but 'took care of their districts'. Here in the Southeast, the Traditionalist elders sold their votes literally for bacon. Why do you think you see so many pigs down here? Everywhere else pigs are taxed to high. The Traditionalist elders sold their vote. Earmarks. Legal bribery. Whatever you want to call it. In the end, the Enlightened got what they wanted. We just need the right candidate to run for PC in the next election."

"You actually believe that myth?"

"Myth?"

Jake expounded, "You think that one man elected as PC can fix everything? That might have been true decades ago, but I've lost faith in the Traditionalists. They will never support a candidate who has moral courage. Rather, your party funds moderate candidates that are palatable to the Enlightened. You guys can't stop compromising. And even if good people are elected as PC and elders, FC's polluted culture tarnishes them. Good elders don't stay good for long. They are sucked into FC's debauchery of power. Well, you were raised in that culture, so I don't expect you to understand."

The Commander sarcastically replied, "If you know so much about politics, tell me... how would you fix it?"

Jake shook his head in frustration.

He's incapable of understanding. He is one of them.

Jake replied, "Sir, let's keep focused on the army of invaders at the bottom of the hill."

The Commander's frustrated tone evaporated, "I agree. We can talk politics later. I'm interested in hearing your suggestions on what to do with the invading horde at the bottom of the hill."

The question caught Jake off guard.

"Ahhh, well, sir, we can't surrender. If we do, we might as well lay out a red carpet to FC. We can't fight. They'd destroy us in battle. We can't negotiate. We have no leverage and I don't trust them. In all of those scenarios the transgressors will have a free pass at FC. Then your family name is destroyed."

The Commander added, "And your family, along with the Continent, will be threatened."

Jake smiled.

This politician has potential. He's willing to wear set of reality glasses.

Jake asked, "Sir, how rusty is your history?"

Intrigued, the Commander grinned, "I love history."

The healer continued, "Two decades after the Savage War, the southern empires overran our legions in the fog. The slave armies streamed north into the Great Rolling Hills to overrun Avanoor before the reserve legion could mobilize. Do you recall what Servius did with the remnants of the legions that were destroyed in the fog?"

The Commander answered, "He used guerilla tactics to slow the invaders' advance. He bought time for Avanoor to mobilize their reserve legion. Hmm. I'm intrigued with your idea. But who is our reserve legion? FC has slashed funding for the legions over the last decade. What's left is nothing close to a reserve legion capable of defeating the transgressors and the multiple waves that are inbound. And most importantly, the PC wouldn't send anymore if he had them."

"Sir, you probably aren't too savvy on how the legion works."

The Commander smiled.

Jake continued, "My father is the head protector of Avanoor. He's friends with many head protectors around the Continent. And I'm not sure if you're familiar with protectors, but most of them are veterans. Most of their father's bled together during the Great War. And trust me, these guys not only stay connected with each other, but they are active members of their local veterans club. I'm talking about a networked brotherhood of tens of thousands of former legionnaires. Sir, the Continent's veterans are our 'reserve legion'."

56

The Commander leaned forward. He placed his chin in his right hand and stared intently at Jake.

The Commander questioned, "So, our reserve legion is an army of grandpas?"

Jake smirked, "My older brother recently left the legion. He's one of those veterans. So are thousands of others like him that are well under thirty years old. And yes, some veterans may leave retirement and polish the rust off their swords."

The Commander smiled, "Nothing would strike more fear into my soul than facing a legion of angry young men led by veterans of the Great War."

Jake added, "Once a legionnaire, always a legionnaire. My father would not hesitate one second to pick up his sword if his nation needed him. So would tens of thousands of his brothers across the Continent."

The Commander sprang to his feet and held out his hand to shake.

He said, "Jake, it's time for you to write the most important correspondence of your life. We'll seal it in my family's coat of arms. I'll have my strongest horse and my personal aide deliver it to your father."

Chapter 10

Federal City

Two hours of "serving tea" to the PC and a few elders remained before Jenny could return home. Over the preceding couple weeks, she acclimated to her initial frustration of not doing anything related to the medical practice in her healer residency. Years ago, she dreamed of putting her years of healer school to use helping others. Now, she was nothing more than a high-level tea server standing by in case the PC needed medical attention. Ironically, the PC was always the healthiest guy in the room.

To pass time, Jenny daydreamed about her recent visit to the historical sites of her new home. Federal City was located in the humid subtropical south central region of the Continent. The city was built not far from the capital of one of the old southern empires.

Two decades after the Document was written, the fledgling nation repulsed the southern empires' invasion force. Jenny visited the location where Crassius defeated one of the emperors. A white marble statue of the legendary Avanoorean stood in the historical courtyard marking the war's turning point. She felt a strange connection to those locations.

She knew why.

She visited the restored emperor's palace and visited the museum that documented the way of life those oppressed peoples endured as mere slaves. Jenny's daydreaming was cut short when the General walked into the office.

The General glanced around the room of elders, advisors, and the PC.

The PC smiled, "General! So nice to see you. Congratulations on subduing the transgressors."

The General bowed and replied, "Sir, thank you. I've come straight from the field. I have some news…for you."

The PC nodded, "Everyone, please excuse us."

He looked at Jenny. She looked back at him.

The PC said, "You stay. Bring the General some tea."

Jenny said, "Yes sir."

Everyone left except for Jenny. The PC and the General sat down on a couch. Jenny brewed a fresh pot of white tea.

"So, General, I'm eager to hear of your success."

"PC, sir. It is…"

The General's beady eyes focused on Jenny as she poured tea into two mugs.

The PC acknowledged the General's concern and said, "Oh, she's fine. She's one of my personal healers and my best tea girl. Don't worry, she's harmless."

The General added, "And she is a beautiful thing, isn't she?"

The General smiled at Jenny.

She cringed.

Creep.

"So, General, tell me the news."

"Sir, if I may, the transgressors aren't like the Pancho Bandits we faced last year in the Southwest. We're facing an entire army."

Jenny nearly dropped the tray of tea. She struggled to not physically react.

Jake.

The PC nodded.

Appalled at the PC's lack of reaction to the news of an invading army, Jenny forced a smile as she handed the men mugs of white tea.

"Would you like honey or a lemon?"

The General waved her away. The PC shook his head.

The General said, "Sir, the initial reports of success that we 'subdued them' were necessary. The Continent doesn't need a panic. You don't need the political fallout. My legion was nearly overrun.

If it wasn't for the heavy rain and mud, they would have defeated us in battle. Our intel indicates that more waves of transgressors are about to hit our shores in the Southeast. What nearly defeated our strongest legion was just the first small wave."

The PC replied, "General. I'm assuming these transgressors are indeed from the southern continent's Kingdom of Anic as was originally reported?"

"Yes sir."

The PC stood up and walked over to his desk. He slammed his fist onto the polished cherry veneer.

"I didn't think he would react...react like that."

The General asked, "Sir, react to what?"

"My dear uncle and trusted friend, please do not repeat the words I'm about to say."

The General affirmed, "On our family's name."

The PC continued, "As you know, we borrow most of our money from Anic. What is unknown to everyone, except a few of my closest advisors, is that we stopped paying interest to them years ago."

The General's jaw dropped, "H...h...how did you—"

"The Right to a Healer was more costly than original estimates along with my other social programs. Uncle, we have been out of money for a while. If it wasn't for the newly discovered gold and silver mines in the Southeast, we'd be bankrupt. With this drought and weak economy, our tax revenues are at record lows. I've already redistributed the wealth from the rich. I'm out of other peoples' money to spend."

The General quipped, "Not one Enlightened thought it'd be possible to defeat the rich. But, my genius nephew, you did it. I am proud of my brother's son. I wish he was here to see your great successes."

The PC ignored the General's bootlicking.

The leader of the Enlightened returned to the couch and said, "Now, I didn't think the king of Anic would react like that to my request to borrow more money. Even with the new gold mines, we don't have enough to fund the Right to Eat. He understands the importance of this right. It needs to be passed. I made it clear that after we implement the Right to Eat, more jobs will be created, our economy would rebound, and our tax revenues will increase. I promised him we'd follow through with all of our financial obligations after I signed the right."

Jenny controlled herself. She directed every ounce of energy into acting oblivious. She focused on washing dishes and silverware. Cleaning up after the PC and his visitors was another one of her collateral duties.

The General said, "Well sir, I don't know what to say. Anic will defeat my legion soon. They may already have. I placed that young Traditionalist in command."

The PC smirked, "Clever. I'm glad I appointed you as general of the legion. You not only think like a politician, but you know what moves to make. Placing a Traditionalist in charge of a 'simple cleanup' mission that will fail…that's astute."

The General asked, "What do you plan to do, sir, about the invasion?"

"I know the king of Anic personally. The people of Anic adore me."

"But sir, I must admit, invading the Continent is quite bold. If he wanted to talk, I'm sure there were alternatives to invasion. As a backup, I can have two reserve legions mobilized and deployed around FC in a week. Even that may be insufficient depending on—"

"No! We're not sending anymore legions anywhere! That snake Traditionalist commander will take the fall. Our talking points will be 'We are flabbergasted that a Traditionalist failed at a simple cleanup mission'. And just because I said you think and act like a politician doesn't mean you'd make a good one. There's a reason why I've conquered the Traditionalists. There's a reason why I was able to do what no other Enlightened PC has done before. The Right to a Healer, Saving the Clouds, and now we are so close to the Right to Eat. We Enlightened have known since the end of the Savage War that Servius's Document proved inadequate to assure us equality and happiness. With my New Rights, the birth of an era of social justice is upon the Continent. I'm the only Enlightened PC in two hundred years that succeeded with implementing our remedy for the Document's inadequacies."

The General stood, bowed, and said, "Yes sir, you are the greatest Enlightened."

The PC paused. He looked at Jenny diligently scrubbing dishes. She appeared inattentive. The PC turned back to the General.

Calmly, the PC said, "There is no need to send more legions. The King will listen to me. This is how he operates. The invasion is his negotiating strategy. It's his leverage—scare tactic. He won't annihilate his debtor. We owe him too much money."

The PC quietly contemplated the situation. The clanking sound of Jenny, standing on the balls of her feet, sliding a dish into the cupboard broke the silence.

The PC smiled, "General, this is perfect. That Traditionalist commander will fail. Then, after speaking to the King, I'll stop their invasion—single handedly. The upcoming elections will be a shellacking. Just imagine what we can do if the Enlightened are in complete power of Elder Hill. We can implement the remaining New Rights and fundamentally change the Document and the Continent for good. Our power will be unbreakable. This is the perfect storm."

Jenny walked over with two plates of strawberry cake and said, "Sir, some fresh dessert from the bakery."

The PC smiled at Jenny and said, "For two hundred years the Enlightened have relentlessly pursued what I will accomplish in one decade. I will transform the Document with the New Rights. And now, upon realizing that I will be the culmination—the greatest Enlightened—a lovely women hands me a plate of my favorite dessert."

The PC gently rested his hand on Jenny's wrist, "My adorable tea girl, I'll be sure to find a place for you in our newer, better government."

Jenny forced a gleaming smile, "Thank you, sir."

She couldn't wait for her shift to end. She was already transcribing, into her memory, a note to her father.

Chapter 11

Light snow peppered Fletcher's face. Riding his horse, he galloped through the waist high grasses of the Great Rolling Hills. A bright ray of sunlight sliced through the clouds illuminating his path. Fresh autumn air soothed his lungs. His sword was latched to his saddle. A long hollow metal tube was tied next to his sword. Winston galloped alongside. The faithful friend disappeared as he dove through a thick layer of grass. He sprang back out.

Everything felt surreal. Fletcher could feel the rumbling of thousands of galloping horses behind him. He gripped the saddle with both hands, turned his head, and looked towards the thundering sound to his rear.

Blackness.

He felt a warm tongue on his cheek. Winston stood on Fletcher's bed. His front paws pressed against his chest.

Fletcher patted his best friend and said, "I know, I know, I have to go too. Give me a second."

Fletcher sat up in his bed and squeezed his eyes shut. Winston gingerly leapt to the floor.

That dream…why is it coming back?

Fletcher rubbed his eyes waiting for his conscious self to completely reclaim his drowsy body. The fresh memory of the dream faded.

Someone pounded on the front door and yelled, "Wake up Fletcher!"

Kinton banged on the door again, "We leave in ten!"

Fletcher shouted, "Give me a minute."

The chief of New Avanoor jumped out of bed and threw on a shirt and pants.

He opened the door and said, "Kinton, what time is it?"

The protector stepped inside and replied, "Almost lunch. Long night?"

"It's been a long few days. I got back after midnight."

Winston limped outside to find a bush.

Kinton replied, "How are the new guys?"

"The sheep are in good hands. Gust and I need this break."

Kinton said, "Hey, that one creator I told you about is testing her invention. Thought you'd be interested in joining."

Fletcher tied his boots and asked, "Which creator?"

"The black powder one."

"Good."

Kinton added, "Throw down some breakfast, take tea to-go, and head to the north fields. You're going to fire one."

"I'll pass on breakfast—don't want to miss this."

Winston returned and curled up on his dog bed.

Fletcher scratched Winston's head.

"You good boy?"

Winston nodded.

"Alright, I won't be long. Stay home. You need the rest."

Winston replied with a disappointed whine. The two men departed.

Fletcher and Kinton mounted their horses and trotted down the street towards the north fields. Fletcher squinted. His eyes slowly adjusted to the bright summer sun. New Avanoor bustled with life.

Blacksmiths poured cast iron into sand molds. Heat emanated from a furnace as a young apprentice pumped a man-sized bellow fueling the fire with air. The pounding of red hot metal from another blacksmith echoed around the neighborhood. The wind carried the chatter of a bazaar selling fresh fruits, vegetables, and grains from two blocks away. Fletcher enjoyed the ubiquitous aroma of freshly baked rolls and sweet cakes.

Hunger pangs roiled his stomach.

The two men trotted past construction workers stacking baked clay bricks. Behind the future housing development a large tank on top of a tower caught Fletcher's eye. Steam and smoke poured out from two small chimneys next to it.

Fletcher pointed at the tower and said, "Kinton, indulge me."

"Ha! It's called a water tower. It's still experimental. You'll have to meet that innovator soon. His name is Newcomen. The guy is so fixated on his grand idea of providing gravity powered water to homes, via pipes, that he overlooked one important factor."

"What's that?"

"Filling the tower with water. Paying someone to haul buckets of water isn't realistic. So guess what this guy did? He invented a machine that uses pressurized steam to turn a wheel to operate another machine that can push water through hoses. He calls the contraption a 'steam driven pump'. He did all of this while living in FC. Predictably, his steam powered machine was outlawed—too dirty, too much smoke, and too many safety concerns with the pressure. So, he moved his steam contraption and pump north."

"Interesting…gravity fed water systems."

"Fletcher, the town you founded has created a bubble of freedom and liberty. Millions of people across the Continent are suffocating from the Presiding Chief's regulations and taxes. It's not natural for taxes to control every aspect of our lives. It's not natural for the government to mandate that everyone must sacrifice so much for the 'common good' or else face a new tax. Who gains when everyone sacrifices for everyone else?"

Fletcher replied, "I know, I know. We've had this conversation a million times. The government gains."

Fletcher and Kinton maneuvered their horses around two dogs sleeping in the street. They watched a couple boys, standing near their sleeping pets, playing catch in the mud with a brown leather ball.

Kinton continued, "The Enlightened believe that the government can solve all problems by mandating, regulating, and taxing. They believe that a 2,000 page law, signed with the PC's magical pen, can fix any societal problem. They think they can create systems that make people happy."

The chief added, "In reality, the PC and his pen outlawed the 'pursuit of happiness'."

"Fletcher, there is a pent up energy of millions of citizens who want to ride horses, own land, raise livestock, start a business, and invent new contraptions—pursue happiness. But they can't. Their hands are tied. Your New Avanoor is the release valve. All of that free-will energy has found the new land of opportunity. A new home. Anyone can come here and use their God given talents to pursue their dreams, innovate, and create. They can start businesses and exercise their entrepreneurial dreams without facing an impenetrable wall of Federals, incomprehensible tax codes, and regulation. They can afford to own land. Farmers don't have to surrender their livelihood because a minnow is threatened by low water levels in the irrigation system. These people have an instinctual drive to improve their lives. They want to raise their children in a better world. And that world is New Avanoor."

Fletcher interrupted, "Don't we turn left here for the north fields…or has that changed too since I've been gone?"

"Good catch. Anyway, in FC, entrepreneurs have to run through a tiger infested jungle just to complete the paperwork to request permission to pursue their dreams. And after running the jungle, laws that 'protect the common good' block their dreams. Look at Newcomen—he was nearly arrested for his steam powered contraption. Too unsafe. Too dirty. Too dangerous to the clouds. Too 'unhealthy for the common good'. You know Creator Eli, right? He's been here for a couple years."

Fletcher replied, "Yes, he showed me his cotton machine last year. Have you seen it operate? The thing removes seeds out of cotton probably a hundred times faster than a human."

"I've seen it. And I've seen his new mechanized cotton spinner. FC forbade him from registering that idea too. 'It would kill jobs'. Do you know how many cotton seed separators and spinners would lose their jobs if FC allowed Eli to commercialize a cotton gin and mechanical spinner? Do you know how many water men would lose their jobs if Newcomen succeeded with his water tower?"

Fletcher chuckled, "It's sad that our hunter-gatherer forefathers didn't outlaw farming. Do you know how many hunters lost their jobs when ambitious men began planting crops and raising livestock?"

Kinton shook his head and said, "Fletcher, the human innovative spirit is flourishing again like it did two centuries ago. The fundamental principles of historic Avanoor, stifled by FC, have been reborn. Man is free to choose his path and convert his time, sweat, and God given talents into something tangible—a better life for himself and his children."

Fletcher added, "Except he has to relocate to the inhospitable Northern Territory."

A sharp crack reverberated from the north. Dogs barked, birds darted out of trees, and the two men held on tight as their horses reared. A black puff of smoke drifted over the northern fields. A curious sulfuric odor intrigued the two men.

Fletcher stated, "I hope we didn't miss the main show."

"No, it's just getting started."

New Avanoor's head protector and chief trotted to the hilltop. Fletcher stopped. Kinton rode a few paces past Fletcher and then looked back.

"What is it?"

Fletcher didn't respond. He looked past Kinton. His eyes concentrated on the bottom of the hill. A dozen people stood behind someone laying on their chest facing down the field. A long metal rod pointed out from their shoulder.

Down the field were two hay stacks with black sheets draped over them. One stack was thirty paces in front of the group of spectators. The other was a hundred paces out. Everyone in the group held their hands over their ears.

Another sharp explosion snapped from the person lying on their chest. Fletcher patted his horse.

"Relax, it's ok buddy."

A thick cloud of black smoke billowed out of the end of the metal rod. The person lying on their chest removed a small pink cushion from between the butt of the rod and their shoulder. The creator stood up.

Long dark brown hair flowed past her shoulders. She turned around. The two leaders of New Avanoor atop the hill caught her eye.

Kinton waved to Fletcher, "Come on. I'll introduce you to Sofia."

The two men trotted down the hill. The group of spectators turned around as Sofia walked towards the men on horses. She used both hands to hold onto the heavy long rod of metal. Fletcher and Kinton dismounted from their horses.

Kinton smiled, "Fletcher, this is Sofia. And Sofia, I'd like you to meet Fletcher the Great."

She held out her hand and smiled.

Fletcher shook and chuckled, "Haha, Fletcher the Shepherd is more accurate."

Sofia added, "The legendary shepherd of New Avanoor. Nice to meet you."

Fletcher blushed. He scratched the back of his head as he looked down at his feet.

Kinton said, "Ignore Fletcher's humbleness. Modesty clouds his ability to understand that he's a myth across the Continent."

Sofia added, "Mythical indeed. My father spoke of you a lot. His dream was to migrate to your city."

Fletcher smiled, "I just work here. Where is your father now?"

"He passed away last year."

Fletcher's smile faded, "I'm sorry."

Sofia maintained her smile and replied, "Don't be. FC should be sorry. They sapped the energy out of his soul. But now, I'm sure, my father is happily looking down on us."

Sofia handed the black smoke contraption to Fletcher and said, "This was his baby."

The end that was placed against her shoulder was wood. The other end was the long hollow metal tube. The barrel was warm and reeked of sulfur.

Sofia added, "This is as advanced as he got it. Since owning swords and arrows are illegal in the Continent, his invention would surely be outlawed. Imagine if the Federals discovered that his creation could bite like a sword at the range of an arrow? They'd lock him up for years."

Fletcher asked, "Did you work on this with your father?"

"No, no. I was a surveyor in FC."

"Surveyor? Why did you leave the good life?"

Sofia replied, "It didn't feel right. I saw what happened to my father. What a man does in his life...his purpose...it defines him."

Fletcher sympathetically shook his head.

Sofia took a deep breath and said, "But I left FC for many reasons. One, because people can't be fired. A coworker of mine couldn't survey her way out of a paper bag. If they let her do actual surveyor work, she'd screw it up and we'd have to fix it. The boss couldn't fire her. So, they paid her to sit idle. She'd show up to work and sit in the lounge getting paid to twiddle her thumbs. Do you know how damaging that is to peoples' dignity and spirit?"

Kinton added, "That's a leading cause of mental distress—getting paid to do absolutely nothing."

Sofia continued, "It's like that one boss we all had that made us stay late one evening for no reason other than to have us there in case he needed something. Imagine that stress, but everyday all day. You were a legionnaire. You know what I'm talking about."

With the back of her hand, Sofia bumped Fletcher's chest.

Fletcher nodded, "Of course, 'that' boss is in every organization."

"But my coworker...FC stole her life purpose. She was paid to do nothing. Sure, it sounds good at first. All she did was eat, sleep, show up, and demand more. She developed several psychological conditions, like burnout and panic attacks. And FC paid her more with disability! After five years she accomplished NOTHING. Do you know that feeling you get after a hard day's work? That satisfaction of accomplishment? She never felt that. And I'm sure you can guess how the rest of us surveyors reacted after watching her receive more benefits than us, and we were the ones carrying the load."

Sofia raised her voice. Emotion flowed out of her lungs.

She stepped towards Fletcher. She jabbed her index finger into his chest and said, "Do you know what Fletcher? God put each of us here for a reason."

Amused with her passion, Fletcher smiled and stopped paying attention to her words. He listened to her energy. He watched the fire blaze inside her heart.

But it was brighter than most others. Sharper. More attractive.

Fletcher looked into her oval brown eyes. He saw focus. Strength. A pure spirit. No fear. Eye lashes. Long eye lashes. Long brown eye lashes. Beauty.

"Take a man's head off..."

Those words jolted Fletcher out of his daze.

He asked, "What? Say that again?"

Sofia repeated, "The weapon you're holding has no accuracy. The one over there can take a man's head off at over a hundred paces."

"I thought you said this weapon I'm holding is as advanced as your father got?"

Sofia pointed towards the firing spot and said, "I did, but the one over there is our breakthrough. I owe you a 'thank you'."

"Thank me for what?"

"This advancement was done in New Avanoor...with the help of some funding."

Fletcher turned to Kinton and asked, "Funding?"

Kinton replied, "Do you remember the tariff on imports you wanted a few years back to fund the protectors, infrastructure, roads, and a few other basic necessities for New Avanoor?"

"Yup."

"Well, our coffers are overflowing with money. Too much revenue."

Fletcher asked, "And you're using extra money to fund weapons development?"

"Well, yes and no."

"Yes and no?"

Kinton answered, "Well, at first, not all of the excess cash. I put some of the extra money in the bank for a rainy day. For the other extra money, we created an investment sharing program. If a business needs funding, we'll match their investment one-to-one. Up to a certain amount, of course."

"Interesting. Who else have—"

"The water tower and a few others."

"How do you decide who to choose?"

"It's more of a judgment call on my part. Obviously, we protectors want the latest and greatest weapons. Also, with the water tower, if Newcomen can make his steam powered pump work, all of New Avanoor could benefit."

Fletcher replied, "Good, but let's not get too carried away with this. And let's lower the tariff. It exists only to generate the minimum funds necessary to properly enforce the principles in the Document."

Sofia interjected into the tangent, "Ahem."

Fletcher's mind had shifted to an entirely new topic—New Avanoor's budget. It's something he hasn't thought about since Protector Kinton started managing the daily operations of New Avanoor's government the previous year.

Sofia knew what to say to recapture Fletcher's attention.

"Chief Fletcher, do you want to fire the weapon that can take a man's head off at over a hundred paces?"

"Definitely."

The three individuals strolled towards the firing area while chatting.

Kinton turned to Fletcher and said, "I have more news for you too."

"About the budget?"

"No. But we found some candidates to be New Avanoor elders."

The three stopped at the shooting area. Sofia picked up the improved weapon.

Fletcher asked, "How about chief? We've been looking for one for how long?"

Kinton replied, "Well..."

Sofia nodded at Kinton.

I got this.

She heaved the improved weapon into Fletcher's free hand.

Sofia said conclusively, "You'll remain the chief."

Fletcher awkwardly stood there speechless holding two weapons—one in each hand.

Kinton stated, "And Fletcher, don't give us that 'I've been chief for five years. It is time for someone else' excuse."

Fletcher said, "Ok, ok. So, sure. Me as chief for the first year or two was fine. New Avanoor was just a small hamlet. And, Kinton, you've been the acting chief when I'm out with my sheep. But come on guys, New Avanoor is three times larger than Avanoor—my hometown. We need experience. Where in history has a chief, of such a large town, been younger than forty years old?"

Sofia said, "That's easy. Young Crassius was chief, well, the acting emperor of both southern empires before he was thirty. Servius, at a young age, took over after Chief Duranto died. And Chieftess Kamila was well under forty."

Fletcher replied, "I mean, in normal times. You're citing examples of the founders. Name a chief in the last hundred years that was under forty."

Kinton added, "This isn't normal times. New Avanoor is its own sovereignty—"

Fletcher changed the subject.

"Sofia, explain to me how this weapon can take a man's head off at a hundred paces."

Sofia and Kinton nodded in concession.

She answered, "Alright, so my father's original weapon is just a long tube with a strengthened chamber and a wood butt. Inside the chamber, the black powder ignites, detonates, and propels a small round lead ball out the tube. You with me?"

Fletcher replied, "Yeah, sounds basic enough. How does it ignite?"

"With a flint."

"How did your father discover black powder?"

Sofia yanked the improved weapon out of Fletcher's hand and laughed, "Haha, long story for another time—Mr. Twenty Questions. So, in the old weapon, the ball had to be a loose fit in the tube or else it'd jam from the black powder's residue. Consequently, after it's fired, the ball bounced around the inside of the tube making its trajectory unpredictable after it left the barrel. It's not very accurate as you can see by the haystack thirty paces away."

Fletcher asked, "How did you solve the accuracy problem?"

"Two main improvements. The first was in the tube. We scratched spiraling groves into the inside of the barrel."

Sofia removed a conical shaped lead ball from her pocket and said, "The second improvement was in the ball. As you can see, we retooled it into a cone-shaped projectile."

Sofia dropped the lead bullet into Fletcher's hand.

She continued, "The base of the projectile was designed to expand at ignition. As it expanded, the lead base engaged the spiral groves spinning the projectile. Similar to an arrow, the spin makes it go straighter and farther. Hence, a first-timer, like you, should be able to take a man's head off at a hundred paces."

Fletcher said, "Let's do this."

Sofia loaded a paper-wrapped black powder cartridge into the muzzle of the tube. She rammed it into the chamber with a long narrow stick. She instructed Fletcher to drop the conical ball into the tube. He did. She rammed it. She handed the weapon back to Fletcher.

Sofia said, "Lay down, cock back the flint, and aim. When you're ready, squeeze the trigger. And here's a cushion for your shoulder."

Fletcher smiled, "I'll pass on your pink pillow."

He laid on the ground and pointed the weapon towards the haystack a hundred paces down the range. He cocked back the flint and stared down the barrel of the exotic weapon. He envisioned the haystack as a pack of wolves—the ones that shredded Winston's leg. He imagined himself lying on the open plains in a sea of grass.

A gentle breeze cooled his face as sweat beaded on his forehead. He felt comfortable—strangely comfortable.

Fletcher held the wood butt of the weapon snug against his shoulder. He squeezed the trigger.

Pain shot through his right shoulder. His ears rang. Sparks burned his right hand. Black smoke stung his eyes. He ignored it all.

He focused on the haystack. He watched yellow splinters spray out of the newly torn hole in the black sheet.

Nice.

Chapter 12

Jake and Arlo shuffled through the stifling afternoon humidity. Sweat trickled off Jake's chin. The blazing sun roasted the two healers as they stepped out from the shadow of the forest canopy.

They found the pond.

The flat surface of the crystal clear turquoise-hued water glistened in the sun.

No ripples. No movement.

A thick forest surrounded the pond. It was a random location for an awkward looking watering hole. No streams or visible water sources drained into it. The shore wasn't mud or dirt. It was rock. The pond's deep area was ten paces from the shore. The dark blue hue of the water spoke of the depth.

At the shoreline, Arlo placed his hands on his knees and hunched over the water. His reflection stared back at him.

Arlo said, "I've been dreaming of a moment like this for weeks. This pond, this cool fresh sweet water, it's so beautiful. I'm about to get on my knees and kiss its smooth glass surface."

Jake smirked and asked, "Where's the ring?"

Confused, Arlo tilted his head.

Jake said, "Yeah, the ring. You've been talking about this pond more than your girlfriend. Go ahead—don't let me interrupt your proposal. Your girlfriend will understand."

Arlo punched Jake's arm.

Jake shoved Arlo and said, "Last one in!"

The two healers, no older than twenty-five years, stripped down to their under garments. They raced into the pond like young boys— young carefree boys, with no worries, nightmares, or anguish.

They welcomed anything that shifted their minds away from the horrors they endured over the previous month. Their first bath in over five weeks was their escape. This pond was their psychological oasis.

The two healers scrubbed more than just weeks of sweat, blood, and grime off their skin. The cool pure aquamarine water cleansed their minds. It soothed their souls.

After washing in the knee deep water by the shoreline, both men floated on their backs. They patted the cool water and pushed themselves to the deep area.

Three days earlier, after making camp, the Commander authorized the healers to take a few hours off to locate and use this bathing hole that the locals recommended. However, Jake and Arlo declined the offer. Their self-imposed ethos required them to sponge bathe the wounded legionnaires and prisoners first.

They lived the healer code—others over self.

Jake inhaled and spun over on his chest. He dove under the surface and swam towards the bottom of the deep section of the pond. He stopped halfway. Pain stabbed his ears and head. The deeper he went, the sharper it pierced. He pinched his nose, shut his mouth and eyes, and blew hard. The pain disappeared. The pressure in his head equalized. It felt as if water flowed through his ears.

The clattering sounds of the pond caught his attention. It sounded like dozens of fish and crabs were repeatedly dropping small pebbles onto rocks.

Jake ventured deeper. The pressure rebuilt in his head as he shivered in the colder water. His eyes focused on the dark blue sand bottom—ten more paces to the floor.

He stopped. A gentle current of icy water stung his torso. He searched for the source of the underwater stream.

His jaw dropped. Frigid water flowed into his mouth.

This isn't a pond...it's a spring and massive underwater cavern.

Jake's curiosity yanked at him to swim into the exotic underwater world. Floating in weightlessness, he decided against going further.

For the first time in a month, he felt at peace as a school of fish fluttered in front of him. They blocked his view of the cavern. Each fish was no bigger than his hand. The blue-gray color of their apple seed shaped bodies contrasted with their lemon colored tailfins. Three yellow diamond spots lined across their bodies.

Jake swam towards the fish and reached out. His hand parted the school in half. The two groups darted towards the cavern and morphed back into one school.

Jake's lungs ached for air. He looked up at the ceiling of his peaceful underwater discovery. He expected to see Arlo floating on his back.

He wasn't there.

The sun faded as a blanket of clouds drifted overhead. Jake darted to the surface. His lungs burned. His vision grayed. His head broke through the ceiling. He inhaled the humid sticky air. Water drained over his face blurring his vision. The peaceful feeling of weightlessness faded.

His moment of peace had ended.

Arlo yelled, "Jake! Come out slowly."

He heard other voices in a familiar tongue.

The sharp ends of two spears hovered inches from Arlo's face. He stood knee deep in the water next to the shore. He held his hands over his head. Two transgressors, holding the spears, had joined him in the spring. Four other transgressors remained on the rocky shore.

The leader of the group yelled, "Come out. Hands up!"

Jake swam into the shallow area, stepped onto the rocky bottom, and waded out with his hands behind his head.

The leader ordered three of his men, "Get them dressed and tie them up. We're taking them back."

The two captured healers threw on their uniforms. The transgressors tied their hands and pushed the two prisoners through the forest back to an open field. They strung collars around their necks and leashed them to horses.

The head transgressor asked, "You are healers?"

Jake replied, "Yes, how do you know?"

He pointed at a patch on the shoulder of Jake's bloodied uniform and said, "Your insignia. The winged caduceus intertwined by serpents. We need healers."

Jake replied, "My wounded legionnaires need me."

The transgressor chuckled, "Not anymore."

Those words ripped the air out of the two healers' lungs. A morbid feeling clamped their hearts.

The transgressors headed towards the legion's camp. The moving horses yanked the leashes tied to the healers' necks. They reluctantly followed.

The transgressor continued, "You people are so arrogant and naïve. How did you ever become so powerful? You think we are dumb? You think we don't know what you are doing? You think we'd invade your anemic country without studying your legions, your tactics, and your history?"

The transgressor spat at Jake's feet, "After the mud prohibited us from destroying you, your commander only had one logical option."

Jake failed to hold back his seething anger. He refused to accept the fate of his wounded legionnaires. The anger boiled into a rage.

Jake shouted, "You hell bound savages, they were unarmed."

He sprang at the lead transgressor. His leash yanked his head back. His body flew out from underneath him. The transgressors laughed as Jake crashed onto his back. He choked and gripped his collar.

The transgressor said, "You two are lucky you left for this pond when you did. We didn't keep many alive. You belong to us now."

Arlo asked, "How…how did you know what we'd do?"

The transgressor rolled his eyes, "We knew you wouldn't surrender, ask for truce, or fight. We thought you cowards might retreat. However, our king's conjecture proved true. You'd utilize your mobility to stall our movement. You'd strike us from a distance at sunset, then run and keep harassing. Just like your Great Servius did to the southern empires two centuries ago. We know your history. Oh, and your messenger..."

A dense pit of anguish amassed in Jake's stomach.

"Your messenger has two arrows in his back. We foresaw everything you did. Our scouts had their eyes on you as your legion fled from that hill under the cover of darkness. We let you slide out. We wanted you to believe we didn't know your plans."

Jake gripped his collar and wrenched at the knot.

The transgressor asked, "What happened to your nation? As a young child, I learned about your mythical legions, your victories in the Great War, and the immense power of your people. I'm laughing now. You are a joke. Mud. Mud saved your sharpest legion from slaughter. No, that's wrong. The mud only slowed the inevitable. Did you think you could actually run, hide, and attack us like your Servius did to those stupid invaders over 200 years ago? We know your history better than you do. And sloppy. You tried to make it look like you were retreating back to FC. My blind and deaf cousin could have seen it."

Jake itched the skin underneath his collar.

The transgressor continued, "Anic will own FC in a matter of weeks. We will sack Avanoor by fall. Then my king will cement his name into Anic's history books."

Jake loosened the knot on his collar.

The transgressor warned, "Don't even try it."

The invader readied his spear to swing. Jake slid the collar over his head. He sprang forward at the armed transgressor. The invader swung his weapon at the healer's head.

Stars flashed in Jake's vision. His limp body flopped onto the ground. He teetered between the conscious and unconscious worlds.

"Sir, he's dangerous. I'll run my spear through him."

The lead transgressor negated the request, "The king wants healers...living healers."

Jake felt two hands grip the back of his uniform. The transgressor flung Jake's body over the back of a horse. Green colored stars flashed through his blacked out vision. He blinked his eyes and patted the back of his ringing head. His eyes slowly focused on the green grass.

The lead transgressor said, "But I don't want him conscious."

Jake cringed.

Blackness.

Chapter 13

"Halt!"

Thomas Longfellow smiled his pearly whites and waved. He galloped past a protector and an enraged Federal demanding he stop.

Longfellow wiped white foam off his horse's neck and said, "Almost there fella."

He looked back at the two men. He waved again. He could still hear them.

The Federal screamed at the protector, "Why didn't you stop him! That's the second one this week!"

The protector replied, "How do you expect us to enforce Horse Tax violators if you Federals don't let us own horses?"

Except for the Federal's screaming and cursing, the conversation grew muffled.

Thomas's thoughts quickly drifted to his home, father, and three brothers. He wondered if they were alive. He was glad he said goodbye to his family that fateful night. He reflected about his father's first reaction.

Outrage.

A lot was at stake—the family business, name, and his career.

His father didn't want to see his son's life thrown into a garbage heap because of a note. He didn't want the golden Longfellow name tarnished.

However, seeing the dead legionnaire in the tool shed and reading the note convinced his father to give Thomas his blessing.

The sister rode with Thomas the first few days. A father and four brothers were not going to let their little sister be around when the Anic's arrived. Thomas dropped her off at their cousin's secluded hamlet far away from the invading Anic's path to FC.

Longfellow snapped out of his thoughts.

Avanoor was right in front of him. Or at least, he thought it was.

He rode through the ruins of the disintegrating gates. He stared at the crumbling walls.

This can't be it.

He didn't care. His horse needed water. The beast stopped sweating not long after waving at the outraged Federal.

He scanned the town for water. Trash and filth cluttered the streets. Weeds and vines were the only occupants of most stores and many earthen homes. The only beauty was the network of gardens—endless gardens people relied on to survive. Each family required around four acres of land to subsist.

This impoverished community was nothing new. It reminded him of his own hamlet and nearly every town he's galloped through.

He rode through a residential area. Hearing the rare sound of hooves, people stepped outside of their homes to witness the oddity. Others looked up from tending their gardens. A scared mother chased her carefree children into their dwelling. She turned and glared at Longfellow.

He smiled and waved.

The scowls no longer bothered Thomas. Residents in every town assumed he was the occasional outlaw on a horse.

Longfellow ignored the stares and continued riding down the street searching for water. His eyes fell on the protector's shoddy earthen one story office. He headed directly for it.

Thomas dismounted the horse and walked inside. A man his father's age sat at a desk. He had just started reading a letter. The envelope on the desk caught Longfellow's eye. The return address was FC.

The man looked up from his letter and stated, "I hope you have a license for that horse."

Thomas replied, "No, but I need to find Head Protector Willard. Is he here?"

"Who is asking?"

"I'm Thomas Longfellow from the south. I carry an urgent message—"

"Longfellow? Like the jewelry maker?"

"Yes…silversmith."

"Well, Longfellow, I hope that message is worth it. I'm sure you're aware it's a felony to violate the Horse Tax."

Thomas reached into his pocket. He withdrew the bloodied Anic arrow and dropped it onto the desk. It rolled off the table and into the man's lap.

Longfellow said, "Greetings from Anic."

"What—"

Thomas cut in, "That arrow killed the original messenger of this note…a note from the Southeast. It was written by Healer Jake Gallatae."

"Who did you say?!"

"Jake Gallatae…the son of—"

The man sprang to his feet.

"I'm his father, Head Protector Willard Gallatae."

The silversmith sighed in relief. Longfellow handed him the note—mission complete.

Willard feared the contents of the correspondence. He hesitated before breaking the seal.

Thomas looked down as he relaxed. His eyes focused onto Willard's desk and the opened envelope. It was addressed from his daughter—Jenny Gallatae.

He chuckled, "Your children like writing you."

Willard asked, "Why is the Longfellow seal on the note?"

Thomas replied, "Sir, it's a long story."

"Well, first, that horse needs water…and to go behind the building out of sight. Second, don't sigh too much. If this note is what I expect, your duty is far from over. And finally, yes, my posterity love their parents."

Chapter 14

"The Continent will endure until those on Elder Hill realize they can bribe the public with the public's money."-Old John

Federal City – Presiding Chief's office

Jenny scanned the rectangular conference table. She recognized most of the faces. The ten leading Enlightened elders sat around the polished oak table. The PC sat at the head. No Traditionalists were in attendance.

Another closed door meeting, like usual.

Each elders' tea mugs were full. A slice of lemon rested on top of the ice in the PC's water. His piece of sweet cake had nearly vanished. The health conscious PC only ate one serving per day.

Jenny sat in her usual chair in the corner of the room dreading another long day of serving beverages and snacks. She flipped through FC newspaper. She read the main headline.

RIGHT TO EAT UNDER ATTACK: TRADITIONALISTS TRY TO OUTMANEUVER ENLIGHTENED

Jenny rolled her eyes.

How? The Enlightened had a super majority up until a month or two ago.

Jenny scanned the next headline.

DON'T SUCCUMB TO DEBT HYSTERIA

Jenny read the first few lines.

Ignore the Traditionalists who fear monger. Spending more than we have is safe. Large deficits and debt are not dangerous. They are actually necessary for a strong economy.

She scanned the third headline and the first few sentences.

HOW BIG IS OUR CONTINENTAL DEBT? *We had more debt during the Great War than today. Nothing catastrophic happened. Our economy actually experienced decades of unimpeded growth after the Great War. High debt is safe, perfectly normal, and actually healthy.*

Jenny's blood pressure spiked.

Jenny read the authors' names. They each earned PhDs from FC's elite universities. One of them worked in the previous PC's cabinet. Another is an "esteemed professor."

Jenny smiled and appeared calm and relaxed. She succeeded in training herself to hide her perpetually distressed inner Heartless. Recently, she's even received compliments on her tranquil demeanor while reading the paper. What they didn't see was her inevitable ball of anxious frustration twisting her stomach.

Jenny folded the newspaper and dropped it on the floor. She took a deep breath, closed her eyes, and exhaled. Her blood pressure settled.

She glanced at the table. Everyone's tea was still full. However, she noticed something different. The elders looked desperate.

Very desperate.

The awkward small talk had ended. The PC wanted to get to business.

Jenny listened.

The PC said, "I've been in a continuous state of bafflement at why we don't have the votes. We have a strong majority. Help me out here, Bertha."

The leader of the Lower Half of Elder Hill replied, "Mr. PC, I ensure you that we will have the votes by next week. We just——"

"You don't sound like you will. Slinging bull at me is futile. And I'm tired of excuses. It's been over a year. How many times do I need to remind everyone that WE control both Lower and Upper Elder Hill? The Traditionalists can't stop us."

A male elder stuttered, "Sir, ahh, they can stop us. They broke our super majority in the Upper Half with the special election two months ago."

The PC stood up, slammed his hand on the table, and yelled, "You are ALL forbidden from speaking of that disaster!"

The PC paused. His eyes locked onto another elder ducking behind Bertha.

The PC glared at him, jabbed his finger, and said, "You! Brains go a long way in this race and guess what? You're running backwards. How did YOU let a Traditionalist defeat our candidate in the most Enlightened part of the Continent!? I will not forget about YOUR incompetence."

The PC sat down. The cringing elder stared at his own cold clammy hands resting on the table.

The PC shook his head in disgust and said, "I'm surrounded by ten idiots."

Elder Bertha asked, "You mean nine idiots, sir."

The PC snarled at Bertha, "No, ten."

The PC's eyes dropped to his plate. The cake was gone. Not even a crumb remained.

He turned around and looked at the young female healer peacefully sitting in the corner.

Jenny stood up and asked, "Yes sir?"

"Jenny, another piece…no. Bring me two."

Jenny replied, "Sir? You told me only one per day—"

"You heard me. Two pieces. Now."

Jenny sprang towards the kitchenette.

The PC turned back to the humiliated elders and said, "My tea girl is more valuable to the Continent than you circus animals."

Jenny bit her tongue as she sliced into the cake. She laughed in her head.

That's the first time I've ever agreed with the PC.

The PC's tone shifted to optimism and said, "Now, don't you all go and hang yourselves just yet. We can still pass the Right to Eat. It doesn't matter that we lost super majority control of the Upper Half. They already passed it. That's why, Bertha, the heat is on you to ram the Upper Half's proposition through the Lower Half."

Bertha said, "Yes sir."

The PC asked, "How many votes short?"

Bertha replied, "Three Enlightened, sir."

"Ahh good. It was five last week. How did you whittle it down to three?"

Bertha answered, "Ah, sir. I did what you told me."

"Good. We won two easy votes. You see? Cutting off irrigation water to farmers last year for that fish gave us leverage this year. Leverage over two elders. Water for a vote. See how easy that was? I hope you people are taking notes on how to control others."

Another elder said, "But sir, if we open the gates to the irrigation canals, the brown spotted minnow population will suffer. Then the chinook sturgeon and green salmon will starve because they rely on the minnows for—"

The PC interrupted, glared at the elder, and said, "People bring joy to this office, some when they come in and some when they leave. Guess which column you are in?"

The elder sat motionless and stammered, "Uh, uh—"

A bulging vein on the PC's forehead pulsated. His skin grew deep red.

The PC clenched his fists and raised his right arm.

He pointed at the elder and screamed, "Get out! Get out of my office!"

The elder scurried out. The door shut.

Silence.

The PC opened his hands flat on the table—palms down. He closed his eyes, filled his lungs with air, and held it in for a few seconds. He exhaled. The pulsing vein relaxed.

The PC opened his eyes, looked at Bertha, and asked, "Who are the final three 'No' votes?"

Elder Bertha's voice cracked as she dropped three names.

The PC shook his head and said, "I'm not surprised. Well?"

Elder Bertha blankly stared at the PC.

He asked, "Well, Elder Bertha, you're the Speaker of the Lower Half. What is your plan or do I need to spell it out for you again?"

Bertha stuttered.

"Bertha, your incompetence makes me nauseous. There are undiscovered tribes in the southern continent—untouched by civilization—that can squeeze votes out of people better than you!"

Shock gripped her wrinkled face. Bertha's eyes fluttered. Drool glistened on the corner of her lips. Silence echoed through the room.

The PC studied the expressionless elders. He grabbed his second piece of sweet cake with his hands. He broke it in half, shoveled it into his mouth, and chewed. With the back of his hand, he wiped the crumbs from his face.

He mumbled with a mouth full of cake, "That was a joke. Laugh."

The nine remaining elders forced laughs fearing for their professional lives.

The PC pointedly said, "You know, all I see around me are people I want to fire. But I can't. That's the problem with elections—it's difficult to control the results. Now, Bertha, what are you going to do?"

"What sir?"

"If stupidity was a disease. You're the plague. And I'm the cure. What is the first 'no' vote's reason for not supporting it?"

"Ah—"

"Offer him something. Every elder has a skeleton in their closet...or a minnow that is blocking irrigation water and enraging their constituents."

Bertha replied, "Sir, umm, the Upper Half's proposition isn't 'Enlightened' enough for the first 'no' vote. He'll only vote for a universal Right to Eat."

"Well, I agree with him. But this is the only way. A universal right won't succeed overnight. If we pass this Right to Eat, we succeed in cracking open the door. Then over the following years we'll kick it open and pump more legislation through it. It WILL be a universal right—just give it a few years."

Bertha replied, "He understands, but his Enlightened constituents have been protesting on his property, harassing his wife, and threatening violence. They want nothing less than a universal right this year."

"He can be bought. Offer his brother something...an appointment. Come on people, use your creativity. And why are his constituents attacking him?"

Bertha replied, "Sir, there are no more Traditionalists in his district to keep them busy."

The PC said, "Remind me to visit that district. I need to remind those unions of their allegiance to me and my programs. Now, where were we?"

"Sir, you wanted me to offer that elder an appointment."

"Yes, offer his brother something."

"But sir, offering appointments is technically illegal."

"Golly gee willikers, Bertha. Following the law didn't get any of us elected."

The PC dropped more cake into his mouth.

He swallowed and sipped his lemon water.

He asked, "Why won't the other two vote for the right?"

Bertha answered, "Sir, for the second individual...his constituents and their grocery stores were protected by the original Lower Half proposal. We promised the farmers and grocery suppliers in his district contracting rights with FC. The Upper Half's proposition doesn't."

"You're telling me that in over 2,000 pages of the Upper Half's proposal, there's not one bit of language that we can interpret in his favor?"

"Sir, four of our best legists analyzed the Upper Hill proposal and found nothing that—"

"Just tell him we'll reconcile it after the Lower Half signs the bill."

Bertha added, "I did. He doesn't trust us. And he doesn't like you publicly attacking grocery stores and calling them evil rich people looking to squeeze money out of hungry children. His constituents are—"

"He is blocking history. Doesn't he get it?! Promise him a lump sum of money to spend as he pleases in his district."

Bertha looked down and said, "We can't. We can't add anything to the Upper Half's proposal until after we approve it. He knows that."

The PC slammed his fist onto the table. He stood and walked to the window with his hands behind his back. He closed the shades.

Darkness.

The PC stood in a shadow.

He spoke, "Ok people, I hoped it wouldn't have to come to this. Here's what we'll do. We'll pass the Upper Half's proposal without voting for it."

Bertha gasped, "What!? The self-executing rule?"

One elder added, "Deem and pass?"

A third shouted, "The Slaughter Rule!? That's dangerous. It could have serious repercussions on us during the elections."

The PC said, "You know what will have worse repercussions? Not passing any bill!"

The youngest Enlightened elder in the room asked, "What are these rules? How do you pass something without a vote?"

Bertha shook her head in disgust and said, "Slaughter, deem and pass, and the self-executing rule are the same thing. If the Lower Half votes to approve an amendment to the Upper Half's proposal, then the Lower Half deems that the Upper Half's proposal is also approved without requiring a separate vote on the bill itself. All we have to do is ensure the Upper Half's proposition is specified in the amendment. It's a way to streamline the legislative process. The Slaughter Rule helps us get more things done for the people."

The young elder shrugged, "Huh?"

The PC hissed, "Next time, check your stupidity at the door."

Bertha ignored the PC and explained further, "You know all those promises we made in the Lower Half bill? Well, we have to add them to the Upper Half bill. But we can't do that until the Lower Half approves the Upper Half. You with me?"

The young elder nodded.

Bertha continued, "Ok. To get around the rules in the Document, the Lower Half will create a package with all the amendments. Then we vote on the package. After approval we then 'deem' the Upper Half's bill as passed."

The young elder said, "Ahhh, I get it. So, by approving the amendments, we also approve the Upper Half bill without actually voting on it? Why use the word 'slaughter'? Is it named after some guy?"

Bertha dropped her face into the palms of her hands. She glowed in embarrassment that the elder she took under her wing didn't understand procedural loop holes. She was even more disgusted that he continued asking questions.

Another elder chimed in, "We call it 'Slaughter' because that is what we are doing to the Document. Of course, we don't actually use the name 'Slaughter Rule' outside of closed door meetings. When in public we call it 'deem and pass'."

Bertha—with her face still buried in her hands—said, "I can already hear the Traditionalists now. 'The Enlightened have gone from passing bills without reading them to passing bills without voting on them'."

Another elder laughed, "Haa, yeah. I can already hear Hudson exclaiming 'The Enlightened just created their own loophole to the most fundamental principle in the Document.'"

Bertha lifted her face out of her hands and added, "Yeah, Hudson will be all over this like a hound on ground beef."

An elder added, "Hudson is a Heartless nut."

The PC lectured, "Know thy enemy. And don't underestimate Hudson. He's the only thing that's keeping the Heartless alive. And he single-handedly kept the Traditionalists from morphing into Enlightened."

Bertha asked, "Are you sure you want to 'deem and pass'? You're asking us to drink from a poisoned chalice. It's political suicide."

The PC frowned and said, "Of course I am! It's been on my mind for weeks already. Like I said earlier, this vote will open the door. The Right to Eat will clinch this election cycle for us. We'll regain the super majority in Elder Hill. Complete power. Do you people understand? This is history. Progress."

The elders nodded in cautious agreement.

Jenny walked to the kitchenette and sliced two more pieces of cake. She carried it to the PC.

He smiled at Jenny. She returned to her chair.

He looked at Bertha and said, "Ok, send the second vote to visit me privately. After two minutes, he'll support the Upper Half's proposal. I want to avoid using 'deem and pass' as much as you do."

Bertha asked, "How are you so sure you can win him over?"

"He has a thing for young boys. How about the third vote?"

Bertha stated, "Sir, ummm. That is what's been on my mind. Well, all of our minds. Maybe you can clear this up for us. It's about our debt."

Confusion wrinkled the PC's forehead.

He asked, "What are you talking about?"

Bertha continued, "Sir, the third vote said he knows about the debt. He verbatim said, 'I know about the PC's lies.' He told me to ask you about interest payments. Sir?"

The other elders nodded their heads approvingly in support of Bertha's courage to ask the question.

Another elder asked, "What are you hiding from us?"

The PC glanced around. Guilt flashed across his face. The tone of the meeting flipped-flopped. It was the elders' turn to grill the PC.

Bertha confidently said, "PC, slinging bull at us is futile. He threatened to go public. He wasn't bluffing."

The PC shook his head and bit his lower lip.

He admitted, "I don't know how he knows. But…"

He hesitated. Looked at Jenny. Jenny appeared to be daydreaming.

She wasn't.

The PC looked at his elders and said, "I have it under control."

Bertha shot back, "Have what under control?"

The PC confessed, "We haven't paid Anic interest on our debt for years."

Jaws dropped as the words sunk into the elders. Their minds raced as they comprehended the immense magnitude of this fiscal debacle. A verbal explosion shattered the awkward silence in the PC's office. Elders jumped to their feet and pummeled the PC with questions.

"Default? How did this happen? How are you hiding it from the markets? From the world? Why didn't you tell anyone? Why aren't we paying? Where is the money? How much money do we have? How long have you lied? How do you have it under control? If this gets out, we're politically ruined. You are a wrecking ball!"

The PC verbally leashed his elders and yelled, "Everyone shut-up! Shut-up and listen to me! We did not default."

The nine fuming elders reluctantly bit their tongues and sat down.

They were leashed.

The PC calmly said, "The Southeast gold rush. That saved us. We were on the brink of disaster a few years ago. Tax revenues plummeted. The Right to a Healer cost more than we estimated—a lot more. The 'Share Your Excess' tax and the profit quotas worked for a couple years. However, the rich are rich no more. We squeezed them dry. And the 'Save and Create Jobs' programs didn't help with the debt."

The PC paused and picked up his fresh piece of sweet cake. He bit into the strawberry dessert.

Jenny thought to herself about what Old John said years ago. His words replayed in her mind.

There are three groups of people on the Continent. The first two groups—the 'Haves' and 'Have Nots'—are a minority of society. The third group makes up 70% of the Continent. They are the 'Have Some But Want More' group. The 'Share Your Excess' tax and profit quotas will fundamentally change the Continent. The 'Haves' won't exist anymore. The 'Have Some But Want More' will have less and ironically become the new 'Haves'. And the population of 'Have Nots' will double...maybe triple.

Jenny whispered to herself, "Old John was right. Everyone is worse off."

The PC finished the cake. His eyes fell on the second slice of dessert.

He said, "But we did not default...technically default. Instead of interest payments, I gave Anic promissory notes on future revenues of our gold mines."

Bertha opened her mouth.

The PC interrupted, "You all would have done the same as me. There's no point in raising taxes...we killed off the rich long ago. So, I only had four options. One, cut the Right to a Healer and jobs programs. Two, stop paying interest. Three, print more money. Four, do a hybrid of the first three. We all agree that cutting funding to the Right to a Healer and the jobs programs is political suicide. After our fourth round of quantitative easing after the Great Recession, it was clear that printing money doesn't work. That left me with only one option—not paying interest to Anic."

Bertha sarcastically asked, "No wonder why they hit the Southeast. If we won't pay them interest, they'll just take our gold mines instead of your IOUs. And why stop there? Why not take FC?"

The youngest elder asked, "Why not just cut back on payrolls, pensions, and benefits for the government employees?"

The PC's face dropped into his hands. He groaned.

Bertha shook her head and said, "Where have you been?! The last Enlightened PC, Dr. Hellenic, did just that. He cut payrolls, pensions, and working hours."

The youthful elder replied, "Forgive me, but I was buried in the books at legist school in the Northeast. What happened?"

"FC nearly burned down. Riots, fires, and chaos."

The PC lifted his face out of his hands and said, "This is a teachable moment for a future leading Enlightened elder. NEVER touch the pay and benefits of government employees. Never."

Bertha added, "The Purple Monster will end your career, just like Dr. Hellenic."

"Purple Monster?"

Bertha nodded, "That's their rioting color. You NEVER want to see them wearing purple in anger...unless they are attacking Traditionalists."

The junior elder persisted, "So, we're just going to roll over to the demands of these—"

Bertha nodded again, "Yes, we do as they say and in return they keep electing us. Well, they do more than that. They strong-arm the Traditionalists with scare tactics and antagonize the Heartless. They round up people on election day, feed them, and encourage them to vote...for us, of course. And I must add that their violence and radicalism have won us many close elections. Feed the Purple Monster with taxpayer money. Let him drink freely from FC's treasury. Learn that lesson and you'll be a successful Enlightened."

The PC pounded his hand on the table and said, "The public unions are sacred. Got it?"

The young elder nodded.

The PC stood up and continued, "Enough with the teachable moment. The Right to Eat needed to be passed last week. Send the third vote to see me in private too. I'll change his mind in four minutes. It's not wise to even consider blackmailing me."

The elders blinked and stared in bewilderment at the PC. Their facial expressions spoke in unison.

The PC understood their stares and replied, "Anic will not invade FC. This is a political play. We'll let the king of Anic take a little gold, fill his pockets, and scare us a little. Then I'll show him our newly approved Right to Eat along with my charm and more promises. Then he goes home. I'll be a champion for stopping the invasion that a Traditionalist legionnaire commander allowed. We'll clobber the Traditionalists in the elections."

Bertha stated, "But we still owe Anic interest that we can't pay."

The PC ignored her and said, "Trust me. Stop worrying. I got it. Everything will work out in the—"

The PC and the nine elders snapped their heads towards the door. It swung open.

The General stepped inside and said, "Mr. PC, I have some urgent news."

"Go ahead."

"The transgressors have conquered our legion. The Traditionalist commander has failed a simple cleanup mission."

The PC smiled, "It has begun."

Chapter 15

Longfellow pounded on Old John's door.

Willard sat on a bench with his wife on the front porch. His wife's face was buried into his chest—her arms wrapped around her solemn husband. Willard's shirt absorbed her tears.

It pained Longfellow to even look at the distressed couple. Their youngest son was probably dead. Their daughter lived in the path of the invading transgressors.

Longfellow prayed in his head for the protector and his wife. He understood the agony of uncertainty. The fate of his father and brothers had never left his mind and thoughts.

Old John's door swung open. The elderly, gray haired man stepped outside. He scrutinized Thomas's eyes. The energy and aura emanating from the old man forced Longfellow to step back. A breeze of stale air mixed with a sense of wisdom seeped out the door. Longfellow froze as the old man visually examined him.

Old John asked, "Who are you?"

Longfellow couldn't speak, but he felt a strange connection to the old man.

Old John had a presence Longfellow would expect out of a senior elder. He could have stepped out of Avanoor's history books.

Old John asked again, "Well?"

Longfellow pointed at Willard and his pained wife and said, "My name is Thomas Longfellow. I'm with Head Protector Willard."

Old John's face lit up after seeing Willard and his wife. He then grew solemn. His heart sensed their anguish.

"My lovely niece and Willard, please come inside. I just brewed some tea."

Willard helped his wife stand. She held her face down, hidden from view. Tears dripped off her chin. Longfellow followed the two inside Old John's home.

Willard shot Longfellow a look.

Show Old John the note.

Longfellow understood. Willard's wife couldn't endure hearing the note read out loud again.

Old John read the visual exchange between Thomas and Willard. He said, "Young Longfellow, help me pour some tea."

Willard led his wife through the home to the back porch.

Longfellow and Old John walked into the kitchen. Old John took the note and hesitated. He waited for the back door to close. His eyes focused on the broken seal and the LF.

Old John asked, "Live Free?"

Longfellow replied, "What? No, it's my family's—"

Old John interrupted, "It's 'Live Free'."

Longfellow corrected the old man, "No, no. The LF stands for my family name—Longfellow."

Old John stubbornly said, "Live free."

"Sir, respectfully, it's my family seal for our business—"

"No, young man, it means 'Live Free'. Now let me read the note."

Longfellow conceded. Old John lifted the note to his eyes. He squinted. Longfellow bit his tongue.

No use arguing with the stubborn old man. He's probably half senile anyway.

Old John looked up at Longfellow. He scowled at the young man as if he heard his thoughts. He returned his eyes to the note.

Longfellow scratched his head.

Great, he's senile and can read minds.

Old John looked at Longfellow again and shook his head. He then re-read the note.

Old John asked, "How did you get this?"

Longfellow told him the story of that fateful night.

Old John replied, "Longfellow, I suspect you know where to go next."

"Ah, not exactly."

As if on cue, the door to the porch opened. Willard walked inside and into the kitchen.

Willard handed a new note to Longfellow and said, "Deliver this to New Avanoor. Give it to my son, Fletcher."

Longfellow asked, "The Fletcher?! The mythical founder of New Avanoor? He's your son?"

"Yes. He's my son."

In disbelief, Longfellow shook his head, "I thought New Avanoor was just some urban legend—a myth created by the Heartless to discredit the PC's policies."

Both Old John and Willard chuckled.

Willard said, "Disregard the media. They are the unofficial fourth branch of government loosely controlled by the Enlightened. Why do you think we true Traditionalists are called Heartless? And why most people think we are crazy?"

Longfellow nodded, "I understand."

Old John added, "Before you depart to New Avanoor I have something for you."

The old man disappeared around the corner.

Longfellow said to Willard, "Strange old fellow, isn't he?"

"He's a treasure to the Continent and has sacrificed a lot. I have nothing but pure respect for him."

Old John re-materialized as fast as he vanished. He carried a large rolled up flag in both hands. He held it out to Longfellow.

Old John said, "Fly this on your journey to New Avanoor."

Longfellow respectfully declined by placing his hands behind his back, "No, I couldn't take your personal flag. It looks very sentimental—"

"No. You will take it."

Old John unrolled the flag. Longfellow's eyes widened. His jaw dropped.

In the upper left corner of the aged red and white cloth was a blue square. Two white letters were stitched into the dark blue fabric.

LF.

Old John said again, "Your family blood is rich with valor."

Willard also stood frozen in amazement next to Longfellow. They both stared at the old man holding the large blood stained flag. Their eyes focused on the two distinct letters stitched exactly how Longfellow engraves LF into his jewelry.

Old John answered their looks of astonishment, "Over 200 years ago this flag flew in the final battle outside Avanoor's walls. It was one of the historic forty-three flags that flew with Crassius in the final charge that defeated the invaders from the southern empires. The letters 'LF' were stitched by a young legionnaire while he was a prisoner in the southern empires."

Longfellow asked, "How did you get it?"

"During the Great War, I was wounded in battle and knocked unconscious. This flag was used as a tourniquet. It saved my life. The man who tied the tourniquet died."

Old John hesitated.

He looked at Longfellow and said, "The man who died—your grandfather—bled to death while he tied the flag onto my upper arm. He passed away before I woke. He was my brother-in-arms and I am alive today because of him. It was his Longfellow ancestor who stitched the LF into the flag over 200 years ago. This belongs to you."

Old John gently placed the bloodied and torn cloth into the silversmith's hands. It warmed Longfellow's body. Energy flowed into his heart.

Old John said, "It's no coincidence that Healer Jake's message found you."

Memories of the day Longfellow took the legionnaire oath, atop the mountain, rushed into his mind again. He thought of his father and the grandfather he never met.

Old John is right. LF means 'Live Free'.

Longfellow's legionnaire instinct took control of his mind.

He said, "Willard, Old John…I will go to New Avanoor now."

Longfellow looked down at the cloth, gripped it in his hands, and walked towards the door.

Willard said, "Thomas…rest first. We will leave in the morning."

Longfellow stopped in his tracks, "You're going with me? You don't have a horse?"

"That's not a problem. A few Federals in town have horses that I can 'borrow'. And to your question about me going with you…"

Willard inhaled deeply. He turned and glanced to the back porch. He focused on his wife sitting alone under a thick quilt.

Willard said, "No. I'm going to FC."

Chapter 16

"Freedom is never more than one generation away from extinction. We didn't pass it on to our children in the bloodstream. It must be fought for, protected, and handed on for them to do the same, or one day we will spend our sunset years telling our children and our children's children what it was once like in the United States where men were free." -Ronald Reagan

The Northern Territory

Winston sprang through the tall grass and froze after landing next to a thick bush. He poked his nose into the bush's leaves. His head swung left. He sniffed.

Nothing.

His nose pulled right. His legs stiffened. His tail pointed straight into the air.

The scent.

Winston darted into the grass. He disappeared.

Fletcher yelled, "Go get 'em, boy!"

Invisible to Sofia and Fletcher, Winston crashed through the dense underbrush. They could only see the waist high grass shake as the dog bolted through it.

Fletcher said to Sofia, "Get ready."

She asked, "How do you know?"

Fletcher didn't get a chance to respond. The bustling grass exploded as Winston sprang into the air and crashed into a bush. Sofia instinctively swung her invention to her shoulder. A blur of feathers and the squawk of birds erupted from the prairie. Four pheasants bursted into the sky. Three of the birds were dull brown and dirty white—females.

The fourth bird's feathers contrasted in the Northern Territory's blue summer sky. The pheasant's blue-green head glistened in the afternoon sunlight. Bright red skin surrounded his eyes. A solid band of white feathers ringed his neck. His golden brown body and wings shimmered as the creature shot into the sky.

Sofia squeezed the trigger. Her right shoulder kicked back. Her torso twisted. Black smoke spewed out of the muzzle.

Fletcher's eyes locked onto the male pheasant. A cloud of feathers exploded in the powder-blue sky. The bird's limp head flopped to the side. His body spun as it fell. Winston's head popped out of the grass. He bounded through the prairie towards the prize.

Fletcher congratulated Sofia, "Nice shot!"

Winston trotted towards her with the bird in his mouth. She looked down at the dog and smiled.

Winston sat. He dropped the bird at Sofia's feet and looked up.

Sofia turned towards Fletcher. Her contagious broad smile, dimples, and sparkling eyes reminded Fletcher of the day he met her.

Sofia guided Fletcher through Creator Precinct a week earlier. While she attempted to convince him to take her shepherding, Fletcher met Newcomen and toured his water tower and steam powered pump. He met other creators and learned of their new contraptions. He viewed scores of ideas drawn out on paper. He examined dozens of models designed by the inhabitants of the neighborhood.

Fletcher asked them all why they left the jurisdiction of FC.

The creators complained of the suffocating business climate. If regulations didn't stifle their ideas, it was the lack of investment. Small businesses, large companies, and entrepreneurs struggled just to feed themselves and their families. The Share Your Excess tax and profit quotas ate away the extra earnings that would fund the development of their innovations.

100

No one had the funding to invest and develop the creators' ideas. They all had the same story.

Federal City suppressed our ideas.

They spoke of fellow creators that didn't migrate north. Those who remained stopped innovating. They surrendered. The time and risk of pursuing their dreams would not pay the bills.

Chasing their ideas drove some into poverty. Others were outcast from society. Many applied for government jobs. Some of the most ingenious creators worked as street sweepers. Others were landscapers. Most had no choice. They had to pay their bills, feed their children, and house their families.

FC's policies dried and salted the once fertile innovative ground. Creativity stagnated. The driver of economic growth evaporated.

Known to all creators, the legend of New Avanoor was spoken in mere whispers out of fear of the Federals. To creators, New Avanoor was the "Gold Rush" of the Northern Territory.

Fletcher's tour of Creator Precinct opened his eyes to the world's new sanctuary for humankind's greatest wealth—man's innovative spirit.

After the hunting trip, Fletcher and Sofia rejoined Gust with the flock. The sun had set.

A gentle nighttime squall drifted over Fletcher, Sofia, Gust, Winston, the recently hired assistants, and the flock of sheep. Moonlight slipped through a crack in the clouds. The light sparkled in the residual mist from the squall. A band of gray, silver, and white light arched through the heavens—a moon rainbow.

Gust slept silently underneath a thick wool blanket. Fletcher and Sofia sat on the damp cool grass facing the silver arch in the sky. They leaned back against a boulder. Their shoulders lightly pressed against each other. They shielded their bodies from the cool summer night and mist with a wool blanket. Sofia shivered.

Fletcher asked, "Having fun yet?"

"It's peaceful."

He said, "It's a nomadic, solitary lifestyle."

Sofia jeered, "That explains why you needed a tour guide in your own town."

She elbowed him.

Fletcher smiled, "Well, I hope this trip is satisfying your seemingly unquenchable fascination with shepherding."

"There is something special about it. Something pure. Something honest."

"I'll tell you what though…you'll do a lot of soul searching out here."

Sofia leaned against Fletcher. Her head rested on his shoulder.

Fletcher asked, "So, a hundred small pellets? That's it?"

Sofia tilted her head up and replied, "Yup, it was my father's idea—perfect shot for small birds."

"Ingenious. Hitting a bird with one round would be nearly impossible. Kinton is the only man I've seen hit a pheasant with a single arrow. So, how many weapons are you making?"

"A lot. Kinton thought I was crazy to go on this trip with you and Gust for a few days. But my weapons shop can operate without me. We're expecting a lot more orders soon, too."

"How are you getting so many orders?"

Sofia replied, "The day after you met me, I hired three salesmen to travel the settlements scattered in the Northern Territory to display and operate the weapon. And, of course, take orders. Four more salesmen are traveling the Great Rolling Hills doing the same. They should be back soon."

"Hold on. You hired salesmen to carry that weapon south across the jurisdiction line into the Continent?"

"Yup."

"Isn't that a little audacious? If one Federal witnesses a salesman test fire—"

Sofia said, "You haven't heard, have you?"

Fletcher shook his head.

"A lot of towns don't have Federals anymore…just started happening this year. Well, mainly the smaller towns in the areas bordering the Northern Territory. We did our due diligence. We're only visiting towns where the Federals aren't around to enforce FC's laws. And we've found that the townspeople are happy to revert back to the pre-Federal days. I guess you haven't heard about the horses either."

Fletcher shook his head again.

"A few days after the Federals vacated those towns, the residents raced north to purchase horses and livestock from New Avanoor.

And, of course, they returned south over the border with their new goods. We're merely using those same trade routes."

Fletcher added, "And I'm guessing after the townspeople loyal to the Federals started riding horses and eating plentiful beef, their support quickly shifted away from the feds?"

Sofia smiled, "Exactly. Well, there weren't many pro-Federals to begin with in that part of the grasslands."

"So, Sofia. What do you plan to do with your new wealth?"

"Don't jinx me!"

"Come on, you're going to make a killing with your father's invention."

"Honestly, I haven't thought too much about it. I've been so focused on just improving and commercializing the weapon."

"Well, what's your life dream besides completing what your father started? What do you want to do?"

Sofia smirked, "I kinda like shepherding."

Fletcher shook his head and chuckled.

Sofia continued, "Seriously, though. I see so many of my neighbors with great ideas and creations. I work with a great team that's helped me convert my father's rugged experimental weapon into a hot selling commercial product. We can do that again...and again with new inventions of our neighbors. A few of my team members are already talking about starting their own businesses and investing in other creators' ideas. Fletcher, this is only the beginning. You saw Creator Precinct. Even if only one in ten of all those ideas you saw succeed...talk about changing the world."

"Sofia, you've already done it. You just made arrows obsolete."

She blushed, "How about you, the legendary chief of New Avanoor? You can't possibly want to follow sheep around for a few more decades."

"Haha, I would have no problem doing so."

Fletcher fell silent. He gazed at the gray moon rainbow. It glistened brightly in the dark sky.

He spoke, "Besides a large flock of sheep...a farm. I want to farm wheat and maize. Grow an apple orchard. Maybe some almond trees too. And harvest honey."

Sofia asked, "Honey?"

"It's from my childhood. Old John told stories about my grandfather and our ancestors as we walked through his peaceful honeyfields."

"Honeyfields?"

"It's nothing overly exotic. We stack boxes containing bee hives in lush orchards, farms, and fields of blossoming wild flowers—honeyfields. And every honey harvest is different. Various flowers, pollens, and orchards change the taste of the honey. Some advanced harvesters plant special crops solely for the honey. Buckwheat honey is the deepest and most flavorful I've tasted. It's truly one of God's greatest foods. And Old John's honeyfields in the apple orchard was the frequent location of our family picnics during the summer weekends of my childhood."

"Don't the bee's attack?"

"Haha, well, we didn't picnic literally next to the boxes."

Sofia leaned more into Fletcher. His warmth calmed her shivering. She felt secure. Safe. Her spirit felt at ease. Relaxed.

She jeered, "Aww, you're just a little boy in a man's body. You look forward to growing old and picnicking in honeyfields. How cute."

Fletcher blushed and said, "It's a Avanoorean thing. Honey is a strong part of Avanoor culture—"

Sofia interrupted, "You really miss home, don't you?"

"What do you mean?"

"You left Avanoor and look what you did? You created New Avanoor. Kinton even told me that New Avanoor is laid out like Avanoor. The town center is a small building that contains a copy of the Document. The largest flag I've ever seen flies from atop that building."

Fletcher playfully asked, "Since when did weapon creators start psychoanalyzing people?"

"Well, I think it's adorable. FC took from you something you cherished. So you left and built a new one…now that's creation."

Fletcher looked down at the young woman leaning against his shoulder. She stared straight ahead at the moon rainbow.

Fletcher said, "Sofia."

She looked at Fletcher. He caught her eyes.

Fletcher said, "Sofia, my life dream is simple. I want to raise a family. I want to restore Old John's honeyfields. I want to listen to my father tell my children stories of our ancestors and Avanoor's history while picnicking in those honeyfields. But I can't."

He turned away. His eyes focused on the bright gray moonbow arching in the sky. The cool air chilled his exposed face. Sofia continued looking at him.

Fletcher said, "Rather, my father will spend his sunset years telling his grandchildren not about our ancestry and not about Avanoor. We won't be picnicking in a honeyfield. The bees are gone. The honey boxes are rotted. The orchards are overgrown with weeds. Instead, my father will spend his sunset years describing to his grandchildren what it was once like in the Great Rolling Hills when men were free. I dread the day when I look into my children's eyes and watch them imagine freedom. That is my nightmare."

Fletcher paused. Sofia slid her hand into Fletcher's hand.

He continued, "Our way of life is not hereditary. Over the last two centuries, our freedom faced threats in each generation. And each generation fought, sacrificed, and protected that freedom. They handed it down to their posterity. I have nothing to hand down. I'm the last generation. I received freedom and I watched it evaporate. I can't settle. I can't marry and raise a family. I can't explain it, but there's something I have to do first."

Sofia asked, "What is it?"

"I don't know. Whatever it is, it torments me. Perplexes me."

Sofia said, "Fletcher, you've founded New Avanoor. You've done it. Your nightmare is no more. You can raise a family. You can tell stories of New Avanoor and of your ancestors. You will not only hand freedom to your posterity, but you can say that you kept it alive."

"It's more than that. I don't know what it is. I can't describe it. That feeling grows stronger every day. More intense."

"What feeling?"

"My gut. My instinct. It's why I left Avanoor years ago. I fought off all logic. I disagreed with my parents, family, and friends. Old John was the only one. He was the only one to smile when I told him of my decision. That feeling and that pull is why I traveled to the Northern Territory…and I nearly died that first winter. Something pulled me up here. And it's pulling even harder right now."

Sofia saw the strain in Fletcher's face. The internal struggle emanated from his eyes.

"Sofia, the larger New Avanoor grows, the more people that migrate here, the more this town flourishes, the more that feeling inside of me intensifies. It fuels me. It fatigues me. It keeps me up at night. It exhausts me. It keeps driving me. I don't know what God wants me to do. You say it was to establish New Avanoor. Then why do I keep feeling it? Why does it only grow stronger? And why do I keep having the same dream?"

Sofia smiled and asked, "What dream?"

Fletcher bit his tongue.

I'm talking too much.

Sofia acknowledged Fletcher's silence.

She said, "Fletcher, if you want this weapons creator to properly psychoanalyze you, you should tell me about the dream."

Fletcher shook his head, conceded, and said, "Ok, it started after the Horse Tax was approved by FC…before I moved to the Northern Territory. It faded away after I arrived, but it's back. Just in the last couple months."

Sofia asked, "How often?"

"Every night. And every night I see more. I feel more. It becomes more real. Like most dreams, it fades moments after I wake. All I can remember is that I'm galloping on my horse through the Great Rolling Hills. Winston is running alongside me. My father's sword is fastened to my horse. Snow is falling…flakes blowing in my face."

Winston barked. Fletcher and Sofia looked at him. The dog stared at Fletcher. The creature looked strangely focused and serious.

Fletcher said, "Now, if I could only understand what he's trying to say!"

Sofia laughed, "He's got such a personality."

Winston barked again.

Fletcher said, "Come here boy."

Winston walked over to Sofia and Fletcher. He sat and rested his head on Sofia's thigh.

She said, "He likes me more than you!"

Fletcher chuckled, "Na, I think he likes the food in your pocket more than me."

Sofia smiled and playfully jabbed Fletcher in his ribcage.

She said, "Ha…I have no food. Admit it. Your dog likes me better."

She petted the shaggy creature. She felt Winston's warmth spread into her hand. It flowed up her arm.

Sofia said, "Fletcher, when you find out what He has planned for you, you'll know. And you'll pursue it. You'll accomplish it. And I can imagine it. I envision you, many years from now, picnicking in those honeyfields with your parents, wife, and children. The weeds are gone. The trees are in full blossom. The honey boxes are buzzing with bees. You're sitting under the shade of an apple tree listening to your father entertain his grandchildren with stories of your ancestors. You're looking content. Your father is looking proud. I'm imagining it now."

Sofia's voice, her touch, and presence comforted Fletcher. Something about her was peaceful. He listened to her description. He imagined the world she described. He felt the burning desire inside of him to start a family and raise children. But he fought it. He shut it out.

It didn't feel right.

Not yet.

He gazed out to the sky. The moon rainbow disappeared. The air had dried. The damp plains glistened in the moonlight. The clouds had begun clearing.

Chapter 17

Somewhere east of FC

Jake, Arlo, and the Commander kneeled. Their hands were tied behind their backs. Five guards stood around the three legionnaires. The sharpened spears, inches from their eyes, deterred any thoughts of being a hero. All three looked past the spears and up at the king of Anic.

The black haired, olive skinned king smiled. His youthful appearance contrasted with the wisdom and mature confidence in his eyes. His straight greased hair touched his shoulders. His sleeveless brown leather shirt revealed bulging and well sculptured biceps and forearms. Many good years were ahead of the King.

He spoke, "I've awaited years for this day…the day a legionnaire commander kneeled at my feet."

The King stepped back and sat in his wooden throne. He opened his hand. A young servant girl, standing next to his throne, handed him a goblet of mead. The King sipped the beverage.

He pointed at the Commander and asked, "You. You come from a Traditionalist family, don't you?"

The shocked Commander replied, "How...how do you know who I—"

The King cut him off and said, "Know thy enemy. Now tell me. Tell me...what do you know of me?"

The Commander stuttered, "You are from Anic, the land of the southern savages who want to sack our peaceful—"

"No! About me. About my kingdom. About our prosperity. About our way of life. About OUR legions. Our power."

The Commander stuttered, "Ahh, ahh."

"My point. My point exactly."

The King stood up and handed his goblet back to the servant girl.

He pointedly asked the Commander, "Do you actually believe we are 'transgressors' here to pillage the Continent? If so, we could have invaded your nation a decade ago after FC grew complacent. We could have sacked FC then. You may ask 'why'? Why didn't we? Why now?"

Jake and Arlo stared. They couldn't believe what was happening—front row seats to history.

The Commander asked, "What are you getting at?"

"There was no need to conquer the Continent. You spent your wealth on us, on our horses, our livestock, our sheep, and our food. For two years I studied in FC. I became an expert in the Continent, your people, and your culture. I experienced the arrogance that flourishes in FC. And the stupidity. With my own eyes I witnessed your government outlaw horses and livestock to save clouds."

The Commander corrected the King, "No, we taxed the ownership of horses."

The King shot back, "You bumbling idiot! Outrageously high taxes outlaws the very thing it taxes. Ridiculous taxes destroy the right of ownership...the right to enjoy the fruits of your labor. You fools. You fools, outlawing horses literally broke the back of your farmers. I watched them step backwards in time and plow the fields with their own hands. Food surpluses disappeared. Jobs dried up. Families turned to subsistence farming to feed themselves. And I watched FC stifle innovation because it was too dirty, too polluting, too unsafe, or too dangerous to existing jobs. Each invention, each advancement, each increase in productivity killed jobs. Your Federal City declared war on innovation. My neighbor. My neighbor had an idea to invent a contraption that cleaned the seeds out of cotton. He

109

desired to leave FC. Where to? I don't know. He's probably still stuck there trimming bushes or sweeping streets. He knew his idea—if created—would have threatened the jobs of hundreds…thousands of cotton laborers."

The Commander interjected, "You must be aware that our weakened economy couldn't afford more lost jobs. We had to save and create them."

Jake cringed. He couldn't believe it. The Commander sounded like an Enlightened.

The King said, "Obviously, the Enlightened have brainwashed you Traditionalists. The Traditionalists. The one group of elders that could have saved the Continent from spending and borrowing itself into ruin. You Traditionalists capitulated. You capitulated what your ancestors believed in. You surrendered the principles that made the Continent so prosperous, so strong, and enviable. Now look. Unquenchable blinding thirst for power consumed FC. You made promises. You were elected. You spend, spend, borrow, borrow to 'buy' more votes. Grab more power. You are so focused on power; you've grown reckless, arrogant, and complacent. FC reeks of complacency. Now I'm here. Now I'm extending the borders of Anic to your shores."

The Commander shot back, "If you're so well informed of our country, then you MUST be aware that a Traditionalist recently won a seat in the Upper Half of Elder Hill that has been held by an Enlightened for decades. We broke their supermajority. After this election, we will take back the majority of Elder Hill. After we elect a Traditionalist PC, we'll fix—"

"Bull. That's pure bull. That's the elixir you feed the people. Twice…twice in my life you Traditionalists controlled all of Elder Hill and the PC. And yet, yet you fixed nothing. Actually, you worsened it. FC, under Traditionalist control, kept spending the Continent's wealth…wasting your wealth. You kept borrowing from my kingdom. You ignored the ominous shift of your society towards a subsistence based economy. Your population growth has stagnated. A languishing economy is a glaring indication of a society's impending downfall."

The King sipped from his goblet and squeezed the back of his neck.

He said, "Your political system swings like a pendulum every thirty years. The radical Enlightened would gain complete control of FC once per generation. They'd implement a series of entitlement programs. They'd inevitably go too far, and come elections, the pendulum would swing back to the Traditionalists. The Traditionalists would regain control of FC and have limited success at scaling back the damage done by the radical Enlightened. Patiently, the Enlightened accepted this slow progression of 'four steps forward and three steps back'. However, after several of these pendulum swings, the Enlightened finally reached the tipping point. And now here we are. In the last decade, the PC led the Enlightened into a new era of near permanent dominance of FC. The Traditionalists are all but extinct."

The King opened the palm of his hand.

He slapped the Commander and said, "You fools expanded the Right to a Healer! Traditionalists have forsaken the Heartless. The Traditionalists have conceded and joined the Party of Power—the Enlightened. What sickens me is that you miscreants shamefully kept the label of 'Traditionalists'. You're nothing more than weak Enlightened. The story of your once great society is such a tragedy. The once great government of the Continent no longer exists for the people. It exists for the politicians and for the power hungry."

The Commander held his jaw, shook his head, and said, "Not true, not true. The people wanted bipartisanship. We had to work with the Enlightened to get things done for the people. We had to borrow, spend, and improve the Right to a Healer. We had—"

"That's the lamest excuse, the lamest cover for a conceding Traditionalist. 'We had to'. The only thing Traditionalists have done is spat on your founders' principles and joined sides with the Enlightened. You and the Enlightened are the same. You both want power over people."

A few drops of blood oozed out of the Commander's cracked lip.

The King smiled and laughed, "The Continent was founded on liberty and limited government. It has surprisingly survived for over 200 years. That is a fluke. The normal state of human affairs throughout mankind's history is for him to be subject to either anarchy or absolute control by his king. Since I will rule the world and rewrite history, one of my historians will include an insignificant side note about the Continent. It will say, 'There was this little fluke of history that existed for over 200 years, where people were free from control by government and where there was a large measure of respect for private property rights. Anarchy was a foreign concept. But then the Great King of Anic returned the world to the normal state of affairs.' I like that. I might tell my historian to write that today."

The King's smile faded. He stepped closer to the Commander. He pointed at him.

"And you know what? I predicted this over a decade ago. Your system of checks and balances in your government is broke. Tell me; tell me who keeps the three branches of your government in check when all three want the same thing? When they want more power over the people? More control? Tell me. Tell me who keeps FC in check?"

Jake squeezed his eyes shut. The King's haphazard rambling gave him a headache.

The Commander confidently answered, "Elections. We are a representative—"

"Your elections are a joke! There isn't much choice when both choices are the same—the same corrupt power hungry politicians. And elections failed to restrict those disastrous pendulum swings. I could argue that elections enabled the slow encroachment of Enlightened entitlement programs. So, Commander, tell me. If the people can't cleanup FC through elections, then how is FC kept in check?"

The Commander confidently replied, "The nine High Priests. They can rule legislation from Elder Hill as unconstitutional."

The King laughed, "Ha! Ten years ago those priests failed to rule the Right to a Healer as unconstitutional. For the first time in the Continent's history citizens were mandated to purchase something for merely being alive—health insurance. The nine High Priests granted Elder Hill the authority to tax citizens for doing nothing. New taxes for inactivity have been pouring out of Elder Hill since then. The Chief Priest ceded Elder Hill such vast powers that it broke the back of Federalism."

The Commander stared in speechlessness.

The King asked, "Tell me, tell me—how else is FC kept in check?"

The Commander stuttered, "Ahh…ahh."

Jake cringed again. The Commander struggled with basic knowledge of the Document.

Jake said, "Commander, the final—"

The King glared at Jake and said, "Young Healer, do you have something to say?"

Arlo whispered into Jake's ear, "Are you insane?"

Jake ignored his friend.

He confidently said, "Article Five. That's the final check on FC."

A broad smile shot across the King's face.

He said, "Finally, someone with a brain. You healers are one of the few treasures left on the Continent…along with your protectors and legionnaires. I killed many brave men over the previous weeks. I'm saddened. It's tragic your PC and his lapdog Federals forced me to slaughter the few remaining good men on the Continent. I greatly respect a true legionnaire. I cherish your strong history. I revere the strength of Servius, Crassius, and the warriors from the Great War. I'm saddened I had to kill many of their posterity."

Solemn, the King looked down—as if he said a prayer.

His head snapped back up, glared at the Commander, and said, "Your gutless Enlightened General…he left all of you to die. I watched him flee the legion with his tail between his legs. I smelled the fear. I watched the cloud of panic follow him."

Anger boiled inside the King's face. His eyes sliced into the Commander. The King gripped the scabbard of his sword.

Shocked at the King's abrupt flip in mood, the three legionnaires scuffled backwards. The guards halted their movement with a few pokes in the back with spears.

"That General will soon feel the cold of my steel!"

The King paused. His anger quickly dissipated. He released his hand from his scabbard.

He relaxed, shook his head, and said, "But I digress. I digress."

He pointed at Jake and said, "Stand up, young man."

The young healer cautiously rose to his feet. Worry contorted his face.

The King said, "Don't be shy, Healer. Now explain to your Commander what you mean by Article Five."

Jake hesitated.

"Go on, don't be afraid."

Jake stuttered, "Ahh…ahh, Commander, sir. Article Five gives power to Regional Elders to amend the Document. No one in FC can stop it. The PC, Elder Hill, and the nine High Priests are powerless."

The King replied, "Now, Healer, do you think that Article Five will save your Document?"

Jake smiled. He looked at Arlo.

Confusion gripped Arlo's eyes.

Why is Jake smiling? Is this actually happening? Is the king of Anic really debating the Document with us? What's going on?

Jake confidently said, "Yes, I believe it will. The Regional Elders live among the people. They are the people. Most Regional Elders have never stepped foot into FC. The PC's regulations and taxes oppress Regional Elders along with the people. Through Article Five, Regional Elders can place more limits on the power and size of the central government. They are the final check. They can amend the Document with additional road blocks and hurdles making it nearly impossible for FC to repeat the binge in borrowing, spending, and taxing."

A crazed smile shot across the King's face.

He chuckled, "Your optimistic spirit is convincing. But, you overlook the fact that Regional Elders' neighbors and their families are recipients of those entitlement programs and other spending. If they scorn FC, their neighbors and families will surely suffer more. So, young Healer, do you believe the Regional Elders are NOT controlled by FC? By FC's treasury?"

"No, they—"

"The Regional Elders are nothing more than drug addicts craving their next fix from FC. The Regional Elders are scavengers waiting for FC's 'Big Hand' to toss out scraps from the treasury. They are too afraid of losing their financial umbilical cord. Your Regional Elders are bankrupt. They rely on Federal funding. They are powerless. FC's purse has neutered Article Five's check."

Jake shot back, "King of Anic. You may have lived here, studied us, and know our way of life, but you don't fully understand the heart, the spirit, and the blood that flows through each of us. I believe in the Regional Elders. I believe in their hearts. I believe the Treasury won't control the will of the people. I believe they'll see past FC's 'Big Hand'. I believe they will do what is right."

The King of Anic replied, "Bold Healer, I may have believed you two decades ago, but that spirit you speak of is extinct. It's nothing more than a whisper in the night slowly fading into distant memories."

The King snapped his fingers. The young servant girl handed him a bowl of dark purple grapes. The three legionnaires watched him drop a grape into his mouth. He spat the seeds onto the ground.

"Now, I didn't bring you here to listen to me gloat. You are here because I'd like to offer you a new life...a new beginning."

Confusion contorted the three legionnaires' faces.

The King continued, "I need good healers in my legion. And you, Commander, I don't like you. But, you didn't run like the General. You stayed. You even tried to fight. I see potential in you. Plus, Commander, if you want to save your family, you will side with me."

The three legionnaires blankly stared.

"I will own FC in the coming weeks. No more legions stand between me and FC."

Jake interrupted, "How do you know?"

"Ha! Do you remember the Pancho Incident last year?"

All three nodded their heads.

"That was my play. I tested the waters. Do I need to explain any further?"

The Commander shook his head and said, "No. It's clear. You knew the PC would make an extra effort not to repeat the Pancho Incident. You knew he'd withhold more legions for political reasons. Also, it's an election year. You cleverly cleared your own path to FC playing on the PC's predictable nature and the delicacy of an election year."

The King said, "Politics flows in your blood. You just increased your value to me."

The King stood back up and said, "Your PC and Elder Hill will surrender to me. By end of the fall I will own Avanoor. I will rule the Continent—my new kingdom—from that historic town and make FC my private vacation villa. A new age is upon the Continent. I will rule every man, woman, and child. That is Anic's destiny. That is my destiny. I am the next chapter in the world's history."

Jake sneered, "You'll never take Avanoor."

The King ignored Jake, smiled, and said, "Your elders will ordain me 'PC for Life'. Your PC will bow to me. Here's my offer to you. Join me and start anew or become a slave. Like her."

He pointed at the young teenage girl holding the bowl of grapes.

The Commander stalled. He wanted more time—more info.

He asked, "Why…why exactly are you invading? You said earlier that you could have invaded a decade ago. Why now?"

The King answered with a question, "Commander, have you lent money to people before?"

"Ahh, yes—"

The King asked, "What if your borrowers stopped paying you interest?"

Silence filled the air. All three legionnaires knew the Continent borrowed heavily from Anic.

The Commander asked, "For how long have we defaulted?"

"Too long. And after learning of the Southeast gold rush I expected your PC to start paying me interest. But no, he funneled that wealth into his 'Second Bill of Rights' initiative and the 'Right to a Healer'. Instead, he sent me paper notes promising me gold, diamonds, and silver. He has disgraced me."

The Commander smirked at the King, "If the Continent's economy sneezes, your kingdom catches a cold. That's why you kept the default a secret. The PC played you."

The King's face flashed red and filled with rage. Evil possessed his eyes. His left eye randomly blinked. His right shoulder spasmed as his head twitched.

The Commander's chin shivered. His words sparked the King's rage and set off the King's tic.

The Traditionalist Commander bit his lip in regret.

The possessed King yelled, "I am a fair man! I accepted his IOUs for years. I let him convince me to not publicly announce the default. The markets would roil if they knew. He took me for a fool. The PC's arrogance is repulsive. My kingdom has suffered enough. It's your turn."

Saliva formed in the corners of the King's mouth. Beads of sweat glistened on his forehead. Small drops trickled from his chin. He grabbed his goblet and gulped the mead. He slammed the goblet to the ground. He wiped the saliva and mead from his mouth with his forearm. He withdrew his sword and ran his fingers along the flat gleaming iron blade. He stared at his crazed eyes in the reflection. He gripped the sharp blade with his hand and squeezed. Blood seeped through his fingers and down the blade. His eyes beamed with hate.

The King raged, "I will purge the Continent. I will cleanse this land of the Enlightened who have foolishly destroyed their own civilization and threw Anic's economy into a dumpster. I will raze FC. Slaughter everyone in that infested city. I hated living there. I despised those worms. The stench of arrogance scarred my soul. That city reeks of permanent decay…decay. They will learn the power, strength, and genius of this 'savage', of me, who they treated like a rat. They will die wondering how I did the impossible and sacked their great city!"

The King's bloodthirsty rant seethed. More blood dripped from his hand and down the polished blade. He kept squeezing. The legionnaires stared in fright. Jake couldn't believe what he was witnessing.

Jake looked at Arlo and the Commander. Their mouths were wide open. Their eyes radiated with fear of death.

The bi-polar king of Anic slid the bloodied sword into his sheath. His rant burned itself out. The young slave girl ran to him and began winding a white cloth around his sliced hand. The King breathed in and exhaled slowly. He regained control of himself. The insanity in his eyes quickly faded as fast as it consumed his body.

The King calmly spoke, "So, Commander and you two healers. Have you decided yet to join my new kingdom?"

Arlo stuttered, "King, King of Anic. If I pledge allegiance to Anic, will my family be safe?"

The King replied with an awkward smile, "Of course!"

Jake glared at Arlo, "Are you serious?!"

Arlo hid the shame in his eyes, looked down, and said, "Jake, I have no choice. The Continent is doomed. I need to save my family."

The King laughed, "Haha. Smart boy. Now how about you, Commander?"

Shame and fear filled his eyes.

He said, "Jake, I have to do what's best for me and my family too. The King will be the new ruler of the Continent. It's inevitable. My family needs to be on the winning side."

Jake's jaw dropped. Shock filled his heart.

Jake said in disbelief, "Don't do this. That is not our way. We are legionnaires—the protectors of the Document. We took an oath."

The King interrupted, "The healers, the protectors, and the real Avanooreans of over a generation ago were the true strength of the Continent. They didn't desire power and that's why they weren't in power. Your great Servius once said that the Continent will fall when good men do nothing. As the spirit of the legionnaire evaporates, the greatness of the Document wanes…fades. The Document now means nothing. Without great men, the oath is empty. Don't worry though. I will hang your Document on my wall as a souvenir. I'll keep an eye on it."

Those icy words froze Jake's heart.

Arlo and the Commander capitulated without a fight and nearly without a thought. All it took was a crazy rage—an insane rant from a bipolar tyrant.

Jake watched the principles of his fellow legionnaires dissipate into emptiness. The blood his ancestors shed so they could live free meant nothing to them—absolutely nothing.

Jake, still on his knees, felt feint. He slumped forward. His head hung down. He gasped. Devastation tore at his heart.

The King is right. The Continent will surrender.

Jake squeezed his eyes shut. He felt nauseous that his mind spoke those words. He couldn't focus. His vision blurred. He fell into a nightmare…a nightmare he never thought possible.

The King pointed at Jake and said to his guards, "Take that healer to the cages. And keep him healthy. He's too valuable."

Two guards grabbed Jake's limbs and dragged him past the King.

His eyes slowly focused on his two fellow legionnaires who abandoned the oath, deserted their history, and had forsaken the sacrifices of their ancestors who died so that they could enter this world free.

Now they bowed.

Jake's bottom lip quivered. Tears pooled in his eyes. Emptiness poured into his heart.

God, save us.

Chapter 18

Northern Territory - New Avanoor

"By the time you receive this note, I will be in FC. Jenny is there. The transgressors will soon take the capital. They already defeated Jake's legion. Mother is staying with Old John. God Bless her heart. She is staying strong. I've dispatched messengers across the Great Rolling Hills to my old legionnaire brothers, chiefs, fellow protectors, and Regional Elders. We will form a militia legion to protect our homes, families, and the Great Rolling Hills. Regional Elders will convene in Avanoor to exercise Article Five. Come home. Bring a legion...or two. Avanoor needs you."

Fletcher and Sofia cautiously looked up at the stranger.

Fletcher asked, "On my father's note, there is no seal."

Longfellow replied, "Your father said you'd know his handwriting."

The silversmith sighed in relief again at completing his second mission. The note was in Fletcher's hands.

Longfellow then handed Fletcher the broken Anic arrow and Jake's note. Fletcher knew his father's note was real. He believed Longfellow. Yet, his mind raced.

Longfellow said, "I'm sorry—"

"No, no...thank you for delivering it."

Fletcher's stressed face couldn't hide the flood of emotions. His brother might be dead. His father and sister were in danger. His poor

119

mother's heart was in pain. He tried to detach himself from the emotions. He had to clear his mind.

Fletcher asked, "What's your story? Where are you from?"

Longfellow explained the twist in fate of the horse carrying the dying legionnaire to his silver shop. He spoke of his brothers, father, and Longfellow silver. He then dug through his ruck sack and removed Old John's gift. He unrolled it.

The wide eyed Fletcher said, "I know that flag."

"This was Old John's."

"You met Old John? It's coming back to me now. Old John showed me that flag when I was young. You're a descendant of THE Longfellow who stitched the LF while a prisoner in the southern empires? Your grandfather saved Old John's life."

Longfellow nodded.

Sofia added, "Fate works in strange ways."

Fletcher looked into the sky.

Sofia and Longfellow watched the New Avanoor chief stare into the heavens.

She asked, "Fletcher, what is it?"

Fletcher replied with a question, "Sofia, how many weapons can your shop make? What can we do to increase its output? How many—"

"Hold on there Fletch! Too many questions!"

"Sofia, we need your shop...our families to the south need your shop."

Sofia closed her eyes. She began mental calculations of her weapons production factory.

Fletcher turned to Longfellow, "You said you're a former legionnaire?"

Longfellow nodded.

"Good. Don't sigh in relief too much. Your adventure has just begun. Welcome to New Avanoor's legion."

Shocked, Longfellow asked, "You already have a legion?"

"We do now. You and me...and Kinton and Gust. Those two don't know it yet."

Sofia smiled, "I think we'll have more than four after we inform New Avanoor of Longfellow's dispatch."

Fletcher placed his hand on Longfellow's shoulder and said, "We have much work to do, but first you could use a hot meal and your horse could use some water."

Longfellow smiled.

Just like his father.

Fletcher asked, "How long was the ride up here from Avanoor?"

"About a week of hard riding."

"You made good time."

Sofia asked, "Thomas, what does the LF on the flag stand for? Is it your family's trademark for your silver ware?"

Longfellow remained silent as he thought about his father's career and livelihood. The realization that the Longfellow silver shop probably laid in ruins tore at his soul. The master silversmith—his beloved father—may no longer walk on this world. His brothers were probably slaves.

Sofia read his emotions and said, "I'm sorry, I—"

Longfellow interrupted, "No, no. Don't be. The LF stands for 'Live Free'."

Sofia said, "I like it! I'll stamp LF onto my weapons."

Longfellow smiled, "I'd like that…and my father would like that."

And so would my grandfather.

Chapter 19

Federal City

Jenny shyly stepped into the banquet hall atop Elder Hill. A blue dress flowed over her body outlining her attractive curves. Her dark hair glistened from the two hours of work Chloe's friend put into it. Her sweaty palms gripped onto a small blue purse.

Chloe followed Jenny into the banquet hall.

Jenny's roommate giggled, "Careful with my purse! It's not a squeeze toy."

"Sorry, I'm just a little, umm, a little nervous."

"A little!? You reek of it! Don't worry though. A creepy elder gave me that purse last year. It's worth more than six months of my salary. It just doesn't match my dress tonight."

Jenny didn't reply. Distraction gripped her eyes and mind. The crowds of elders, elites, experts, and legists wearing their most formal attire bustled around her. Magnificent chandeliers glistened from the ceiling. The chatter of hundreds of blissful members of the high society jumbled her mind. She felt out of place—uneasy.

Her high heels sank into the soft red carpet—the only comfort she felt.

Chloe said, "Come on silly! I want you to meet someone!"

Chloe grabbed Jenny's wrist and pulled her into the crowd. The two girls weaved around groups of elders holding thin crystal glasses of wine. One beefy red faced elder tilted a bottle of Regal Majesta mead towards his friend's glass.

Chloe yanked Jenny's wrist in a new direction. She bumped into the plump bald man. Regal Majesta mead splashed onto the red carpet.

He turned and snarled, "Watch it! This mead is worth more than you!"

Jenny bit her tongue.

Jerk.

Chloe yanked Jenny in another direction.

Jenny rolled her eyes and said, "Chloe! Where are you taking me?"

"Over here! He said to meet by the fountain."

"Who's 'he'?"

The two young healers weaved through the party towards the back. The crowd thinned as they neared the fountain. Jenny's eyes focused on a lavish silver fountain. A young woman wearing a red robe stood next to it. She held a silver bucket in her hands. Jenny noticed an elegantly shaped 'LF' engraved on both the silver fountain and the bucket.

Jenny said, "Hey, that girl looks familiar. I saw her the day I met with Healer Aaric."

"Oh, her? She's a new healer too, like you, but no one likes her. She's a Heartless."

Chloe scanned the crowd. On her toes, she attempted to peek above the throng of high society.

Frustrated, Chloe said, "He told me he'd be here."

"Who?"

Chloe ignored Jenny and said, "Here, let's get a drink."

Chloe walked to the fountain.

She snapped her fingers at the red robed Heartless healer and said, "Two drinks, now."

The young woman forced a smile and poured wine from the bucket into the silver fountain. Wine flowed out of the fountain's spigot, down a long strand of pearl beads, and into Chloe's crystal. She filled a second glass.

Jenny stared wide-eyed at the spectacle as Chloe shakily handed her a glass.

Jenny asked, "Everything ok?"

Chloe replied, "Yeah, yeah."

She continued scrutinizing the crowd. Her nervousness and frustration evaporated.

Her eyes lit up, "Oh, here he comes!"

A young man walked towards the healers. He smiled after catching eyes with Chloe. He looked at Jenny and smiled again. He then noticed Jenny's purse. He frowned.

Oblivious to the frown, Chloe yelled, "Philip!"

He snapped at Chloe, "What are you doing with that purse!?"

Caught off guard, Chloe stepped back, and said, "Ahh, umm. I gave it to Jenny."

"Bull. You lent it to her because it doesn't match your dress tonight."

Jenny bit her tongue.

Only a man native to Federal City could understand girl fashion.

Chloe defensively replied, "No, well…I was going to sell it. It's worth a lot, you know. I just haven't found a buyer yet."

Philip said, "Whatever. I was going to give you a second chance."

He turned to Jenny, "Do you even know what your roommate did to get that purse?"

Jenny innocently shook her head. She bit her tongue again.

The creepy elder?

Chloe interrupted, "Philip, are you serious?!"

He snarled, "I'm done with you."

Philip disappeared as fast as he arrived. Chloe stood speechless. She lifted the wine to her mouth and gulped. She stepped towards the fountain girl.

"Another wine."

The young woman, in red, slowly lifted the bucket to pour wine into the fountain. Chloe impatiently held her glass under the pearls.

"Just pour it directly into my glass."

The Heartless nodded.

Jenny thought about all of the expensive clothes, purses, shoes, and accessories Chloe owned. She always wondered how Chloe afforded such luxury. She couldn't afford all that on her healer salary. And her father was a poor Grasslander.

Jenny cringed.

How many elders? For how long?

Jenny didn't want to know. Philip only confirmed what she had suspected. Jenny trembled at the thought that many elders, elites, and experts at the banquet were part of the "club." The rumors had to be true. The tacit offers Jenny received from the high level residents of FC were exactly that—offers. It was not just a few creepy elders. It was a network. And it was why all the healers on Elder Hill were attractive women.

Five more years of this? Five more years of serving tea to perverted old men?

Jenny shivered at the thought. She watched Chloe gulp down her fourth glass of wine.

"Ahh, Chloe, shouldn't you slow down?"

"No, I'm feeling better. It's so annoying that guys my age get so jealous that I've dated a few older men."

"Older? They could be your father."

"Jenny…give yourself six months. You'll start dating some elders. It happens to nearly everyone. Come on, let's go meet some."

Jenny held up her hands defensively and replied, "I really don't feel like it. I want to go home."

"Come on. Just hang out with me for a couple more hours."

"No, Chloe, I want to go—"

"Jenny, ok then…just one hour. Please? Just one more?"

Chloe's roommate reluctantly conceded.

Both healers swung their heads to the front of the banquet towards the percussion of a giant suspended gong. On the balcony, a young man—wearing a red robe—swung a massive leather hammer into the bronze gong a second time. And then a third time.

The bustling party of FC's ruling class fell silent. All the chattering ceased.

Next to the gong, the PC walked onto the balcony overlooking the entire banquet hall. The crowd erupted into cheers.

Everyone clapped and started chanting, "Yes we did! Yes we did!"

The PC waved his hand and basked in the glory. Jenny rolled her eyes at the two minutes of cheering, chanting, and hand waving. She looked at Chloe. Jenny's beaming roommate looked possessed.

Chloe said, "Isn't he amazing?!"

Jenny blandly replied with her rehearsed answer, "Yes, he is. It's so wonderful that we are on the cusp of making history and passing the Right to Eat."

The Presiding Chief spoke, "A decade ago Elder Hill joined together and overcame incredible odds. A decade ago we accomplished what the Enlightened have dreamt of doing for the last one hundred years—the Right to a Healer. After the historic success, I signed the right into law. At the last election, the people of the Continent came together and demanded more change. They demanded more rights. After the election, Elder Hill strengthened with more Enlightened representation. And I was re-elected.

"And during the previous year the Enlightened on Elder Hill again battled the Traditionalists over the Right to Eat. We fought those who believe in the status quo. We clashed with the irresponsible and those who wish to violate everyone's civil rights. The Enlightened defeated the party of 'No'. We again succeeded in progressing our great nation towards the ideals of a perfect Continent. The historic Right to Eat vote on Elder Hill yesterday was the will of the people. The vote yesterday represents what makes the Continent so great.

"Tonight we not only celebrate that historic vote, but we celebrate the monumental act that will occur tomorrow morning when I will sign the Right to Eat into law. Tonight, we celebrate how my signature will change the projectory of history."

Jenny whispered into Chloe's ear, "Projectory? Doesn't he mean traject—"

She replied, "He's so wonderful, isn't he!"

Both healers returned their attention to the PC.

"The Right to Eat is our next crucial step to permanently transforming the Continent! You have embraced my ideals. And embracing me is embracing a larger idea of human perfectibility. Morality is on our side during our voyage of transcending human banalities. Tomorrow we will take a giant leap towards a perfect society."

Cheers, shouts, and clapping erupted. The PC basked again in the applause.

The PC held his hands up to silence the crowd. The cheers faded. He continued speaking.

Jenny ignored the PC's words. She looked behind her at the fountain girl in red. The girl looked emotionless. Powerless. Helpless. She looked like she gave up long ago. Her empty eyes spoke loudly as she held the silver bucket of wine. Jenny saw a broken and lost creature.

Jenny listened to the PC's words.

"Our new rights are for the good of the Continent. Each year we grow closer to reaching social justice. The closer we become, the more wealth our society will create. More equality will lessen suffering. The Right to Eat is a critical step in easing the pain of the children. FC provides healthcare, hence, it's only right that we provide food. By providing food to all, we can ensure everyone eats healthy. A Federal City controlled food plan for the entire nation will complement the great healer program led by my good friend Aaric.

"And tomorrow morning's miraculous achievement will echo around the world. My emissary spoke with the king of Anic today. My message has convinced the King to return his legions back home. And the king of Anic will visit FC tomorrow to witness me signing the Right to Eat into law. He is interested in learning more about our society and our path to perfection and equality for all. Our way of governance is the envy of the world and it will spread to each corner of mankind. We will lead society into a new chapter of human civilization!"

Jenny whispered to herself, "He's going off script again."

Chloe turned to Jenny, "What?"

"Nothing."

Chloe turned back to the PC. Jenny rolled her eyes again.

The PC continued, "The question is, can Traditionalists say yes to anything? Will they join us as we carry society towards perfection? Or will they fight progress? They fought the Right to a Healer and Right to Eat—and we won. They sabotaged the Right to a Home. Fear not, for next year we'll push through a new Right to a Home. We'll call it the Right to Live Comfortably."

Cheering and clapping exploded. The banquet hall rumbled. The PC waved and absorbed the accolades of his followers.

He thanked the crowd, "Please, please, thank you. Thank you."

He continued waving as the banquet hall returned to silence.

"Over a decade ago, in the days of greed and excess, I proclaimed that at a certain point you've made enough money. We

127

acted on my belief. Since then, our great campaign to spread the wealth around is near completion! We have made the people of the Continent more equal! However, it's unfortunate that the policies of the Traditionalists from over a decade ago are still damaging our economy today."

Jenny chugged down her glass of wine.

Still blaming his predecessor after a decade. Unbelievable.

He continued rambling. Jenny cringed and stopped listening. She forced herself to block out the PC's voice. She heard enough of him during her tea duty. She thought about home. She missed her family. She couldn't wait to return to Avanoor for her four weeks of vacation.

Vacation.

That's one right she didn't mind. The PC signed an executive order a year ago making an annual four week vacation a right.

The Right to a Vacation.

Chapter 20

Willard Gallatae rode through FC's gates. He could barely see the transgressors in the evening's twilight. Hundreds of campfires marked their position. The sight of a foreign army at the gates of the Continent's capital sickened him. Yet, he was relieved to see that FC hadn't fallen yet. His daughter was still safe.

Amazed at the complacency of the people, he trotted down the main street of FC. No one seemed worried that an invading force had camped just outside the city walls. They even seemed excited.

Willard shook his head.

He rode past a tea shop with a grand opening banner hanging above the door. He pulled back the reins, dismounted, and tied his horse to a tree. People walking out of the tea shop grimaced at him.

One young man snapped, "Doing that will harm the tree."

Willard walked up to the short scrawny man dressed in bright green and pink clothes.

He warned, "If you were wise, you'd leave this city now. The Anics aren't here to drink tea."

Intimidated by the brawny rough looking Grasslander, the young man squirmed. His tea splashed onto the ground.

He stepped back and stuttered, "I'm... I'm going to get a protector. You're a...you're a stupid Heartless. And you owe me a tea."

He spun around and scurried back to his friends. They walked off into the darkness.

Willard stepped into the tea shop. He withdrew the only note he received from Jenny. The tea barista cringed at seeing the dirty Grasslander.

"Umm, how can I help you sir?"

Willard placed the note on the counter and asked, "May I have directions to this address?"

The barista replied, "Umm, sir. We are only licensed to sell tea. You can receive certified directions from the tourist info center down the street."

Willard shook his head.

The stories of this place are true.

"Son, I'm in a bit of a hurry. There aren't any street signs in the city. Could you just point me in the right direction?"

"Sir, don't you know? They took the street signs down to create and save jobs. Tourist info centers were built and staffed as a result. It's been a wild success. Now, can I take your order?"

Willard shook his head again.

"No, thank you. But how much for the newspaper?"

"Um, sir. Newspapers are free."

"Free?"

"Sir, the newspaper companies were going bankrupt years ago and FC bailed them out. The government now provides free news."

"Ah, I see."

Willard grabbed a paper, turned around, and walked outside. He wasn't fazed that everyone in the tea shop scowled at the awkwardly dressed Grasslander. Willard stopped at his horse. He opened the newspaper and read the headlines under the flickering light of a street lamp.

ELDERS AND PC CELEBRATE RIGHT TO EAT TONIGHT. KING OF ANIC VISITING TO WITNESS PROGRESS!

Willard shoved the newspaper into a satchel on his horse, shook his head, and untied the reins.

He mounted his horse and trotted down the street. He found a tourist info center—a newly built white wooden shack on the street corner. He rode up to the window. He peeked in and heard snoring.

Willard knocked on the window. The snoring stopped. The window slid open. An obese man in his mid thirties poked his head out the window and squinted. His fat rolls hung over the side of his chair. More hair grew on his neck than on his head.

130

The tired portly man asked, "Can I help you?"

"Yes, may I have directions to this address?"

Willard pointed at Jenny's envelope.

The man with no visible chin rubbed his eyes with his round plump hands. His neck fat jiggled as he read the address. Drool dripped from his lower lip.

"Oh, that's just two blocks that way. Make a left and go two more blocks. Would you be interested in tickets to the historic Right to Eat signing ceremony tomorrow?"

Willard replied, "Ahh, no thank you."

Shocked, the rotund man said, "Everyone is going to be there. This is history being made. You can have seats to watching the Continent progress."

The man shoved the two tickets out the window and said, "You want to be there."

"Does it cost anything?"

The pale man laughed, "Haha, no. You Grasslanders are always asking about costs. Is that all you worry about?"

Willard took the tickets and said, "Sir, do you have a family?

"Ahh, yes."

"I strongly recommend you leave that shack right now, pack your things, and take your family north."

The man snorted, "Why!?"

"The king of Anic is here to invade FC."

The man stopped laughing and barked, "You're a Heartless! Give me those tickets back!"

The man's flabby arm shot out the window and ripped the tickets out of the Grasslander's hand.

Willard said again, "I'm serious. For your family's sake, you don't want to be in FC tomorrow."

"Get away from me before I signal for a protector!"

"Signal a protector for doing what?"

"For…for, threatening me, spreading false rumors, and…and being Heartless. I'm going to signal for one now!"

Willard shook his head and rode off. Minutes later he found Jenny's home and pounded on the door.

As he waited, he calculated that it'd take no more than an hour to pack and eat a late dinner before departing Federal City's gates.

If all goes well, we'll be out of harm's way in a couple hours.

Chapter 21

A small hamlet outside Federal City

Jake scratched under his collar. His scraggly two week old beard itched.

It looks like I haven't shaved in over a month.

He gazed upon the capital of the Continent in the evening's twilight. He thought about his sister. He thought about her path in life that led her to be a healer.

Jenny was torn five years ago. She had two desires in life—to heal and to teach. She loved both history and medicine. Both careers were highly honorable and dedicated to serving others in their own unique ways. Jake told her to pursue what was in her heart. However, her heart desired both. How could she know what to do before she was even twenty years old? She followed in Jake's career footsteps and graduated from healer school, however she didn't join the legion.

Jake's thoughts drifted to the note he wrote to his father before the transgressors captured him. The Commander's personal aide volunteered for the mission. He cringed remembering what the transgressor said about the two arrows in the messenger's back.

Jake's eyes focused on FC's silhouette. He imagined his sister in a hospital caring for the elderly, the weak, and the sick. He prayed that she landed a residency in Avanoor. That's what she wanted.

However, if the national healer program was anything like the legion, Jenny was probably anywhere but Avanoor.

I hope she wasn't assigned to a hospital in FC.

He imagined FC's hospitals overwhelmed with combat casualties and wounded civilians. The closer the king of Anic rode to FC, the more his emotional scars from living there opened. The King had grown more unstable over the previous few days. Walking into FC would surely rip those scars wide open. Seeing elders and the elite would pour salt on those emotional wounds. The King would snap.

It was inevitable.

Jake shuddered at the thought of having front row seats to FC's annihilation.

The king of Anic yanked Jake out of his thoughts. The healer gripped his leash relieving the pressure off of the collar around his neck. He gasped for air.

The King said, "Time to win over more of your people."

Jake snapped back, "You won't succeed with this hamlet."

One of the King's guards gripped his spear and thrusted it inches from Jake's face.

The guard pleaded, "Your majesty, no man shall speak to you in that tone. Let me—"

"Silence!"

The King smiled and asked Jake, "How so? Why won't it work? Tell me. And this is why I enjoy keeping you around. I value more than your healer skills."

"This small hamlet overlooking FC is populated with Enlightened. They don't want to be freed. They don't want their horses or livestock back. What you've been telling the previous towns won't work here. They want FC more involved in their lives. They are dependent on FC. They want more government provided rights. And they worry more about hurting the clouds than about those without jobs living in poverty."

The King chuckled, "You persist to underestimate my wisdom. To subdue the enemy without fighting is the acme of skill. And I know my enemy. And I must say, you are partially correct. This hamlet loves the Enlightened and what they stand for. However, I enjoy the pleasure of always being two steps ahead of you."

The King turned to the guard and ordered, "Go tell the chief and elders of the hamlet they are now welcome to join me for some Regal Majesta mead."

The King said to Jake, "Watch me conquer this small hamlet with three glasses of mead, a smile, and a few words."

The guard returned moments later with the chief and two hamlet elders.

The King stated, "Welcome to my camp. Please sit around my fire and enjoy the mead."

The hamlet's leaders politely thanked the King, sat, and sipped the expensive beverage.

The King spoke, "I've been watching the Continent with much frustration. FC crawls like an injured snail carrying the Continent slowly towards social justice for all. I'm here to bring a new era to the Continent. I desire to fly towards social equality like an eagle. What took the PC ten years, I will do in two."

The chief spoke, "We like what you say. However, we hear stories of human rights violations in your kingdom. We believe in equality for all."

The King danced around the accusation and replied, "What you hear are myths. False stories. Don't worry. I will not undermine the basic notions of social justice that you cherish on the Continent. And it's ironic that you worry about my kingdom. I believe the PC hasn't done enough. You should worry about him. And what he has accomplished isn't permanent yet. The Traditionalists could still take back power and stop further progress. If the PC and Enlightened lose the upcoming elections to the Traditionalists, that'll open the door to a new era of irresponsibility. The Continent is at risk of relapsing into an era…an era where the poor are ignored, the elderly are forgotten, and the children starve. Under my rule, that era will remain nothing more than a Traditionalist dream. But most importantly, I'll complete the remaining rights in the next two years."

One elder pointed at Jake and said, "If you believe in equality, why is that gentleman wearing a leash?"

The King bellowed, "Haha! He is a Heartless. That is how my kingdom treats the radical Traditionalists."

The chief and two elders smiled and nodded approvingly.

The King added, "As the new ruler of the Continent, I'm happy you understand that I will not violate your social rights as the Traditionalists desire. I will forbid any Traditionalist from holding any position of power. Do you have any questions?"

The chief said, "We look forward to working with you to usher the Continent into a new era of more rights, more help from FC, and more equality and fairness. What is it that you ask of us?"

Jake couldn't believe it.

Do they actually believe the King? They look possessed. Or are they intimidated and merely feigning everything because the King's army is camped next to their quiet hamlet?

The King stood and said, "Bow...bow to me and pledge your allegiance to me, your new king. Kiss my ring."

Jake watched in horror as another town professed their loyalty to Anic. He watched as three men bowed, kneeled, kissed the ring, and traded the liberty of the hamlet's residents for empty promises.

Jake's soul had been depleted of all emotions days ago. It almost seemed routine to watch his fellow countrymen toss away their freedom so effortlessly.

Some towns just wanted their horses back. Some feared his army. Some were duped into believing the King would restore the Document and the Continent to the way it used to be.

The King played everyone.

Now, the King deceived people into believing he'd outperform the PC in enacting more Enlightened rights.

The King was correct. Subduing the enemy without a fight was the acme of skill. And the King's fluency in that skill was unparalleled.

Jake watched the hamlet's three leaders bow again, thank the King, and walk away. The King turned around.

A glimpse of insanity beamed from the King's eyes.

He said, "All too easy."

Jake trembled.

The King snickered, "If you thought that was entertaining, wait until tomorrow."

Chapter 22

Jenny's eyes had tired from rolling so frequently. She wanted to leave the banquet. Chloe was stumbling drunk. Jenny was sick of listening to elders and the elite brag about their pet projects, spending initiatives, and creative ideas to "better society" or "make it more perfect". She wished she could eradicate the "Good Idea Fairy" that had infected everyone on Elder Hill. She grew tired of hearing the phrases "it's for the public good", "achieve social justice", and "enhances our human rights."

Jenny gulped down her fifth glass of wine. She watched Chloe flirt with a gray haired elder as he bragged about saving the children.

"My program this year spent fifty percent more than last year."

"Well my legislation created or saved more jobs last month than anyone else's."

The lanky bald Traditionalist elder added, "And I supported both of your projects. You know I need support for my immigration amnesty package."

The two Enlightened elders sighed and acknowledged they owed him a favor.

Jenny's frustration boiled beyond her tolerance level. Inebriated, her fifth glass of wine dissolved any remaining self control.

She interrupted the elders, "Sir, I thought you were a Traditionalist? Why did you support—"

The three elders and Chloe responded with annoyed looks.

The Traditionalist elder replied, "Yes, I am a Traditionalist, but I work across the aisle. The people of the Continent want me to be bipartisan."

"But you've completely sold out your principles."

The Traditionalist elder warned, "A wise young woman would keep her words gentle tonight."

Chloe slurred, "Don't mind her. She's new and gets cranky when she's tired."

He looked Jenny up and down, licked his lips, and said, "I like your dress."

Jenny shot back, "But sir, the Enlightened don't compromise their principles in order to be bipartisan. Only the Traditionalists have been compromising. Only Traditionalists have been crossing the aisle. The Enlightened do nothing."

"Well, young lady, someone has to compromise. And don't forget, we are the minority party. We have no control of any branch of the government."

Jenny gulped more wine and asked, "I thought five of the nine High Priests in the Preeminent Court are Traditionalists."

"Not really. As you may be aware, almost any intellectual structure can be built on the sparse words of the Document. And the majority of High Priests interpret this sacred manuscript with deep intellectual thought. But you are correct in that five of them were appointed by Traditionalists."

Jenny replied with a dumbfounded look.

The Traditionalist elder replied, "Young lady, don't worry. Our great party is merely progressing like the Enlightened. We'll eventually gain more seats and take back FC."

The two Enlightened elders chuckled.

The Traditionalist elder replied, "We'll see who's laughing after this fall's elections."

He turned back to Jenny, "What is your name?"

"Jenny."

"Could you use a new pair of shoes? Or how about another purse?"

Jenny shivered.

Creep.

Chloe slurred, "Come on Jenny, you need a new…new everything."

The elder continued, "You can join my staff for my new immigration proposal. Part of the program is to grant scholarships to the children of undocumented citizens."

"Umm, I like my job in the PC's office."

Jenny swigged down more wine.

"Well, I can talk to him and maybe rotate you out of there for a month or two."

"Umm."

Jenny finished her sixth wine.

He continued, "If you're not interested in the immigration reform, my staff is drafting up new common sense measures that will protect citizens from man-caused climatic threats. Next month Elder Hill is scheduled for some robust debate. We'll probably create another bi-partisan committee to decide how to undo the damage man has inflicted on the world's fragile ecosystem. We could use an extra aide."

Jenny slurred, "Doesn't every elder have silly ideas to save the environment? And robust debate on Elder Hill is anything but robust."

The two Enlightened elders gasped.

The Traditionalist elder stepped back and said, "Chloe, I understand your roommate is new and slightly inebriated, but I don't think she understands."

Embarrassed, Chloe stuttered, "Ah...ah...I'll get more drinks for everyone."

She walked off.

The Traditionalist said, "Jenny, your problem is you think like the old Traditionalists. They still don't acknowledge the facts and proven science that our climate needs our help. The kingdoms across the great seas are dirty, polluted, and unhealthy. We need to show them how to create wealth for the common good without polluting the air, soil, and water. We elders can grow the economy and create more jobs through increased spending."

Chloe returned with a tray of crystal glasses filled with Regal Majesta.

Jenny ignored the drinks and replied, "Are you serious?! Elders don't create wealth. Fat governments drain a nation's wealth. The private sector is the real wealth generator. The PC has stifled the innovative spirit of the people. And he's defaulted on our debt."

All three elders glared at Jenny. Chloe gasped nearly dropping the tray full of drinks.

The Traditionalist elder said, "That's enough out of you, young lady!"

Jenny stepped on his words, "True Traditionalists seek only to protect the social contract created by Servius that undergirds our society. We do not hate the government, as you Enlightened did when you were not in power. I love the Continent and the Document. The PC and Elder Hill should comply with the Document, honor our God given rights, and respect our hard-earned private property."

The tray of Regal Majesta crashed to the floor. Jenny felt the expensive drink splash onto her open toes and ankles. Chunks of broken crystal shattered on the soaked red carpet.

The three elders fumed with anger. Chloe's upper lip curled.

Jenny burped, "Look at you all. You elders blissfully drink Regal Majesta while the Continent crumbles."

Chloe gasped, "You're a Heartless! I've been living with a Heartless! You fooled me you evil witch. I want my purse back."

Chloe lunged. Jenny stepped aside as she stumbled into a young man—wearing a red robe—carrying drinks to elites. A half dozen glasses spilled and shattered onto the backs of two cringing elders.

The conversing groups surrounding Jenny fell silent. A dozen people turned and watched the spectacle of Chloe falling to the ground and two elders cursing the young man in a red robe.

Chloe shakily stood up.

Jenny yelled at her, "You're a brainwashed slut!"

She then looked around at the dozens of shocked elders, experts, and elites.

Jenny pointed at them and slurred, "You're all brainwashed. The Continent is bankrupt. FC has burned this nation's wealth. The economy has been a zombie for a decade. We have fallen off the cliff...and will implode tomorrow, next month, or next year."

Half of the banquet hall fell silent. Everyone inched away from her as if she was a contagious victim of the plague. A circle of FC's most powerful men and women, dressed in their most formal attire, formed around the drunk Heartless.

Someone yelled, "Put her in a red robe!"

A few others screamed, "Get her a tray!"

One yelled, "To the gong with her!"

139

The Heartless Grasslander continued, "The king of Anic is not here to watch the PC sign the Right to Eat. He's here to collect years of unpaid interest and principal."

The PC calmly walked out of the crowd and into the open space encircling Jenny.

He said, "Healer Jenny, what is going on here?"

"PC, tell them! Tell them what you and Bertha discussed the other day."

The PC calmly said, "I have told them everything. And it's all in the newspapers."

Jenny boiled with frustration.

By now the entire banquet hall was dead silent. The music stopped. All eyes were on Jenny. Healer Aaric darted through the crowd and into the open space behind the PC.

Aaric pointed at Jenny, "You're fired. Go back home to your putrid grasslands. Return to the Continent's armpit."

The PC turned around and said to Healer Aaric, "Give her one day to pack up and leave."

Jenny shot back, "I only need one hour."

She walked past the PC and towards the crowd. The elites, elders, and experts parted as Jenny walked through them. Her hands were clenched tight.

Chloe yelled, "I want my purse back you tramp."

An elder leaned over, placed his hand on Chloe's lower back, and whispered into her ear. Chloe's scowl instantly transformed into a broad smile. The elder gently squeezed her waist.

Jenny stopped at the door and turned around to face everyone. The crowd stared at her. Jenny wanted to speak her mind, but no words could express her internal storm of repugnance. Only one clear thought formed in her head.

I should've been a history teacher.

Chapter 23

Bright morning sunlight beamed through a hole in the trees and onto Willard's face.

He awoke.

Willard's back cracked as he stood. He walked out of the small forest behind Jenny's home.

He rubbed his eyes.

She's gotta be home by now.

Willard pounded on the door.

Nothing.

He turned the knob. It was locked.

He pounded again and waited.

Nothing.

He walked around to the back. The sliding door was unlocked.

Willard stepped inside.

Nothing.

No smell of breakfast. He walked to the foot of the stairs.

He yelled, "Jenny! Are you there?"

Silence.

"Chloe! Are you there? This is Jenny's father, Willard."

Silence.

Willard walked upstairs.

"Jenny…Chloe? This is Willard, Jenny's dad. Anyone here?"

He peeked into the bedrooms.

The beds were empty. He forced an optimistic thought into his head.

Must have spent the night at a friend's place.

Concern hid behind the optimism. Willard ignored the deplorable churning in his stomach.

She's better than that.

Willard walked outside with a bowl of water for his horse.

"Here you go buddy."

The horse lapped the cool drink.

Willard spoke again to his horse, "How about seeing some history while we wait for Jenny? It's been years since I visited the statue of Crassius."

The horse ignored him. He kept lapping water.

Willard continued, "Well, we got over an hour before Jenny starts work. We'll intercept her there."

The horse looked up and then returned his mouth to the ground to munch on grass.

"You ate enough already. We're going."

Willard mounted up and rode towards the same visitor info center for directions. He expected to see the same obese man. This time he watched a rotund woman squeeze herself into the small white hut. The door closed as Willard approached the window.

She stuck her head out and asked, "May I help you?"

"Yes, directions to Crassius's statue please."

The obese woman opened a map, circled the statue, highlighted the recommended route, and handed it to Willard. Her cheek and neck fat jiggled.

Willard replied, "Thank you."

She stared at him and said, "Hold on. Are you THE Grasslander that threatened my husband last night?"

Willard chuckled, "I believe you have me confused with someone else."

He turned away and rode down the street.

The portly woman shrieked, "Protector!!!"

The high pitched scream pierced Willard's ears.

A protector one block away rode his horse over to the white hut.

The obese woman pointed at Willard and furiously yelled, "He's the violator!!"

The protector yelled, "You! Grasslander, stop!"

Willard shook his head, turned, and trotted up to the protector.

The protector withdrew a flip book from his chest pocket.

He asked, "Your name?"

"Willard Gallatae."

"Address?"

"Sir, may I ask what this is for?"

The protector answered, "This is a ticket."

"Ticket? Ticket for what?"

"Tying your horse to a tree, spreading false information, and attempting to spread panic."

Willard replied, "Are you being serious?"

"Yes. We received multiple complaints about you last night."

The protector scribbled on the pad. He tore the top page off and handed it to Willard.

He said, "Your date in court is tomorrow. See you there."

Chapter 24

Jenny opened her eyes. Curled up on the ground, she shielded her face from the intense sun. Stabbing pain throbbed in her head.

I'm never drinking again.

Jenny sat up. The purse's designer emblem was imprinted on Jenny's cheek. Two leafs were caught in her hair. Her back screamed in agony. Her stiff neck cracked. Her numb left leg was asleep.

Memories from the previous night flooded into her mind. She felt both afraid and relieved. She looked up at Crassius's statue. She stood and smiled. No matter how down or stressed Jenny felt, visiting the statue comforted her. And most Enlightened avoided that historical sight. It was her one bubble of peace in FC—her one escape.

Now it was time to escape FC.

Jenny spoke to the statue, "Crassius, I guess only a few more hours and I'll be out of here."

She opened Chloe's purse.

Good...there's enough cash for a tea.

While walking towards the tea shop, a rugged looking man sitting on a horse next to one of the many info centers caught Jenny's eyes. She couldn't see his face—only his back. An obese woman handed the man a map.

Gosh, that's the first time I've seen anyone use an info center.

Jenny turned down the street towards the tea shop. She withdrew a handful of change from Chloe's purse.

She owes me about five teas anyway.

An ear shattering scream blasted from the info center. Jenny shut her eyes and squeezed her temple.

Oww…I'm seriously never drinking again.

She stepped into the tea shop.

Chapter 25

The late morning sun broiled the sea of humidity encompassing FC.
No breeze.

Crowds of thousands of people packed the road between Elder Hill and the PC's residence. The citizens of FC enthusiastically awaited history. All eyes were on Bertha and her top elders proudly leading the momentous procession down the middle of the road towards the PC's home. Protectors lined the streets keeping the masses from encumbering the swaggering Enlightened elders.

Bertha carried a massive gavel in both hands. A shorter elder walking next to Bertha held a stack of paper—over 2,000 pages—wrapped in leather.

The Right to Eat.

Holding their noses high, they exuded triumph, victory, and undeniable pomposity.

A dozen elders tightly walked behind the two prominent Enlightened elders leading the spectacle. They politely fought to share the limelight and walk inside Bertha's bubble of reveling. Only one more political step and the right would magically turn into law—the PC's signature.

Chapter 26

Jenny looked at herself in the mirror.

She said to her reflection, "That's it. I'm done packing. Time to leave this hell hole."

She slung her bag over her shoulder and opened the door to her home. She tossed Chloe's purse onto the ground.

An overwhelming urge tugged at her. Her stomach and taste buds overruled her logic and desire to escape FC. Her mischievous side allied with her taste buds.

She smiled.

It'll drive the PC insane that there will be no cake awaiting him on his momentous day. Plus, he's at the signing...his office will be empty.

She briskly walked down the crowded street and towards the PC's residence. She headed towards the back entrance opposite to the sprawling crowds.

No door guard? That's strange.

She dropped her ID card back in her pocket and walked down the empty hall. She approached the PC's office. She cracked the door open and peeked inside.

Empty. Good.

She entered and then closed the door. Her eyes locked onto the cake. The PC consumed half of it the previous night.

She reached for the dessert and froze. Footsteps echoed from outside the office as she turned around.

The person knocked.

Jenny remained motionless.

The person knocked again. Jenny held her breath.

The door cracked open.

A man said, "Anyone there?"

Jenny thought the voice sounded familiar.

The door swung open. The man stepped inside.

Jenny's hands flew to her mouth. She gasped. Her wide-open eyes radiated joy.

"Daddy!"

Jenny sprinted to her father and jumped into his arms. She drove her face into his chest. Willard wrapped his arms around his daughter.

"My beautiful princess."

Tears of happiness streamed down her cheeks.

She looked at her father and said, "Daddy, I want to leave. I don't want to be here anymore. Take me home, please."

"My darling, that's why I'm here."

"Daddy, I quit my residency yesterday."

The father and daughter heard two people walk towards the entrance of the office. The door was open. Two men stepped inside the room.

The PC said, "She didn't quit. I fired her."

Chapter 27

Bertha, a dozen elders, and the king of Anic stood on a stage located on the PC's front lawn—the focal point of an ocean of spectators. Jake, still wearing his leash, kneeled behind the King. Tens of thousands of people cheered, hollered, and enthusiastically awaited history.

Jake had the best seat—the best view.

He could barely hear the conversation between the King and Bertha. Then Bertha pointed at Jake.

He inched forward and heard Bertha ask the King, "May I inquire about the bearded gentleman wearing a collar and leash?"

"He's not important. He is what you call a Heartless. But he is a Heartless from my kingdom."

Bertha smiled and said, "I like your style."

The King asked, "Where is your PC?"

"He should be out soon…he is, umm, rarely ever on time."

The King's lip quivered. His voice cracked.

Jake inched forward some more.

It's starting.

The king of Anic said, "Elder Bertha, let's cut to the chase. I'm here to collect from the PC."

Bertha stepped back, "I'm not quite sure I understand. Today is about the Right to Eat."

"I could care less about that. You know exactly what I'm talking about. You owe Anic years of interest and I want my principal."

Jake watched the King's head twitch and his right hand squeeze his left hand.

It's coming.

Bertha said, "But…but after we sign this Right to Eat, it'll fix our economy. It'll be historic."

"Elder Bertha—"

Desperate, Bertha cut him off, "The PC added an amendment that grants all citizens of Anic the Right to Eat while they are on our soil."

The King swiveled his head towards the PC's residence. He saw nothing and clenched both hands.

Bertha continued, "The Right to Eat places a panel of Federals…appointed by the PC…in charge of ALL food purchasing decisions. We can work out a deal with you. We'll buy all our food from Anic."

The King said, "Don't take me for a fool. You already buy most of your food from us. You're out of money. You have nothing to bargain with."

"Not true. We have the gold mines in the Southeast."

The King shot back, "Not anymore. And stop quibbling. I know your type. I lived in FC. You don't care about the people or the Document. You care only about power."

Bertha defended herself, "Well, I don't worry about the Document. I care more about the people dying every day of starvation."

The King jabbed his finger inches from Bertha's face and said, "It's obvious you don't worry about the Document. You ignore what it says about God given rights of freedom and liberty."

Bewildered, the other elders didn't know what was happening.

Bertha stepped away from the King's finger and said, "No, and I believe the Document says we have a right to happiness."

The King laughed, "Ha, actually, no it doesn't. Your Document says you have a right to pursue happiness."

Bertha shot back, "Some unfortunate people are unable to pursue happiness. What we need is equality. Equality is impossible in a free world."

The King replied, "But opportunity is equal in a free world."

"But not everyone can take care of themselves in a free world."

"A very miniscule slice of the population needs help. And in the name of that tiny percentage that really needs assistance…you forced FC onto everyone."

Bertha gasped, "King of Anic! You sound like a Heartless!"

The King's face flashed cherry red. A vein on his forehead pulsated.

Regretting saying those words, Bertha stepped back.

Amazed, Jake couldn't believe the King's self control. He should have popped minutes ago.

The King looked again for the PC.

Nothing.

He turned back to Bertha and smiled, "We duped your PC."

Bertha frowned, "What are you talking about? Who is 'we'?"

"Five years ago, the PC made arrangements with other kingdoms around the known world to rid the planet of legions. Your PC dreamt of a legion-free world. He believed that zero legions translates into zero wars and a safer world."

Bertha said, "I know, I co-sponsored that initiative."

"Not long after that, he stopped paying us interest. Not very wise, Bertha."

She pleaded, "But this Right to Eat will change all that! Trust me."

The King snarled, "It's futile to hold a logical conversation with a blind cat."

Bertha kept her lips sealed.

The King looked again at the PC's residence.

Nothing.

He scowled at Bertha and said, "It's so simple too. To protect your nation, you need legions that can repel your most powerful enemy. It's that simple. However, you taxed, spent, and borrowed your way into a decade long recession. You suffocated your economy. You gutted your legions and ripened your nation for invasion. Your PC has inadvertently beckoned my attention."

Bertha froze. Her jaw dropped.

The King continued, "As the shadow of the Continent's power recedes, the tide of other kingdoms rise. Anic is not the only hungry empire."

Chapter 28

Willard spun around.

He said, "Mr. PC, respectfully, I apologize for intruding in your office—"

The PC interrupted, "Do you know how many laws you've just broken?"

The General walked in behind the PC.

The PC asked the General, "Where's my personal security? I want this Heartless locked up. And his daughter too."

The General replied, "Sir, all protectors and your guards are waiting for you at the ceremony. Remember you sent them—"

The PC snapped, "Yes, I remember."

Willard interrupted, "Respectfully, sir, don't go out there. The king of Anic seeks only bloodshed. I can take you north out of harm's way."

The PC and the General laughed.

The General said, "I should run my sword through this worm right now for treason...for trying to stop history."

Willard replied in defense, "Mr. PC, respectfully, I took an oath to defend the Document and our political processes. The king of Anic is a threat against your safety and the Continent. Please, I implore you—"

The General snapped, "You're lucky we are inside the PC's office. Out of respect for his residence, I won't shed your blood here."

Willard ignored the General and said, "Mr. PC, sir, the king of Anic is unstable…psychotic. You know this. You know him. By walking out that front door, you risk your life."

The PC tacitly agreed with Willard about the King's instability.

The General continued snickering, "Do you actually think you can convince the PC to not sign the Right to Eat after ramming it through a near impossible political process? You are one optimistic Heartless."

Willard continued ignoring the General and said, "Mr. PC, you can sign that thing whenever you want. Just don't walk out there with the king of Anic right now. Why hazard your life for something you can do in safety?"

The PC held his chin and said, "You know, this Heartless does have a point."

The flabbergasted General yelled, "Are you serious sir!? You're not actually listening to this sleaze?!"

Willard added, "Mr. PC, send the General out there. He can tell the King that you are running late or you're ill or something. It'll buy time."

The PC remained quiet.

Willard pointed out the window, "Does that look like a diplomatic party or a force of crazed invaders with blood in their eyes? The King even had the gall to bring a bearded slave wearing a leash! The last time a man wore a leash on the Continent was over two centuries ago."

The PC gazed out the window. Indeed, a kneeling bearded man wore a leash. And the King's personal guards were armed with longbows. Two squads of Anic archers circled the stage. Seeing the leashed man sent shivers up the PC's spine.

He said, "General, I have one more lesson in politics for you. Never risk your own hide when you can risk someone else's."

The General muttered, "You're kidding me! You're going to listen to—"

"Stop the insubordination, General, and walk out there."

"What! Are you serious? I am your uncle."

"And I'm the Presiding Chief of the Continent. Get out there!"

The General conceded and bit his lip.

He asked, "Sir, how long should I tell him you'll be?"

The PC fumed, "Do you want a promotion? Do you want my support for your political aspirations after you retire from the legion? Get outside and deliver the message."

Like a defeated dog, the General lowered his head. He acknowledged that the PC controlled his life and future.

Willard smiled on the inside. He maintained a composed and emotionless facial expression. Jenny lightly elbowed her father.

Nice, Dad!

Hunched over, the General slowly turned around. He straightened his back, took a deep breath, and walked outside.

Chapter 29

Clouds drifted towards the sun. The once idle humid air began gusting. Bertha and the King's passionate discussion fueled the mob of Federals and FC residents. The energy from the ocean of Enlightened spectators magnified. They believed Bertha was schooling the King on how to progress his kingdom.

However, Jake heard every word.

The King spitefully stated, "Don't worry, the Continent will be split up civilly."

Bertha stared in amazement. She squeezed the wood gavel in her hands. The other elders' jaws dropped. They didn't even attempt to hide their expressions.

The King continued, "Over the previous decade the Continent's demand for livestock, horses, and other commodities were fulfilled by all of us 'inferior' kingdoms. Your imports financed our economies. Now you're bankrupt. Our economies have crashed. And now King Zevack from across the East Sea and King Nharim of the empire across the West Sea are most likely on your shores by now."

The hair on the back of Bertha's neck straightened. The short mustached pig-nosed elder bit his lower lip with his buck teeth and shuddered.

The King said, "We are here to collect."

One of the King's guards tapped his shoulder, "Almighty king, someone is leaving the PC's home."

The King grinned, "Ah, finally, here comes the PC."

The look of anticipation on the King's face soured.

He screamed at the top of his lungs, "Curse that General! Where is your PC!?"

The General couldn't make out the King's words, but sensed the tone in his voice. Infuriated, the King eyeballed the General as he walked towards the stage. Jake scratched his beard, smirked, and inched backwards.

The General approached the King, forced a smile, held out his hand, and said, "The great king of Anic. So nice to see you. The PC will be out shortly."

"How does he know?!"

The General withdrew his rejected hand and replied, "Know what?"

The veins on the King's forehead pulsated. His neck muscles flexed. His eyes beamed with malevolence. He ripped his sword out of the sheath. Jake inched further back.

The King screamed, "How does he know I'm here to kill him!"

Holding his hands up, the speechless trembling General stepped back shaking his head. Urine puddled under his boots.

The King drove his sword into the General's chest. He stared into the General's wide eyes. The King smiled as he watched the shuddering man gasp for air.

He kicked the General's body off his sword. He swung his steel at Bertha's neck. The gavel hit the stage. The handle snapped. Bertha's head thumped onto the ground and rolled towards the General's corpse. The short elder with a moustache shrieked.

The King turned to him. The two thousand page Right to Eat exploded as it crashed onto the stage. A gust of wind swirled hundreds of blood sprayed sheets into the air. The elder's pig nosed head rolled into the puddle of urine.

Following their king's lead, the Anic bodyguards and archers slaughtered the PC's personal security and a dozen protectors.

The agile king sprang off the stage and mounted his horse. He gazed into the crowd.

What were cheers had transformed into a frenzied revulsion of what their eyes witnessed. The King pointed his sword at the tens of thousands of people out to watch the Continent progress. Panic rippled through the ocean of FC citizens. The murmur of denial flashed into screams of delirium. The packed crowd stampeded.

Jake considered escaping during the chaos. He tugged at his leash. The guard glared at him. Jake watched an elder fall to his knees facing the King on his horse.

The elder begged, "Please spare me. I will serve you."

The King kicked his heels into his mustang. It reeled. The horse's front hooves landed on the elder. His crying was replaced by the sound of his skull crunching.

The remaining elders dispersed towards the retreating crowd. The King turned to his archers and guards armed with long bows. He waved his hand. They mowed down the running elders. The archers continued launching arrows into the sea of hysteria. Two arrows slammed into an obese man. His portly wife shrilled. She tripped over his quivering body and slammed her head onto the ground. Another arrow flew into her fat rolls on her waist. She stood and started running. Two more arrows sunk into her suit of blubber. She ran like a bull stuck with arrows barreling away from certain death. One of her stumpy legs collapsed and her body crashed to the ground. As she rolled to a stop another arrow dove into her throat and sliced open her jugular.

The King yelled, "Stop wasting arrows on these worms of society. To the PC's residence!"

The King observed four archers dart to the PC's lavish house. He turned his head, caught eyes with his signalman, and nodded.

The signalman lifted a massive red flag and waved it. The King gazed to the east towards his camp. His eyes focused on his legion in formation on the hill. His sharp vision locked onto a miniscule red flag waving in acknowledgment of the King's order. Immediately, thousands of warriors streamed down the bluff and towards the east gate of FC.

Spattered with blood, the King smiled.

Chapter 30

"Mr. PC, we need to leave now."

Willard watched the PC drop his cake into a bag. He sprinted out the back door leaving Willard and Jenny.

Willard shrugged, "Looks like he's going with us."

"Dad...it looks more like we're going with him."

Jenny grabbed her bag and followed her father out the door, down the hall, and outside. The PC had already mounted a horse and dug his heels into the beast. Willard jumped onto his horse. He held out his hand and swung Jenny up behind him.

"Dad, behind us! Go now!"

Willard glanced behind him. Four Anic archers sprinted around the corner of the PC's home. They withdrew arrows from their satchels.

Willard slammed his heels into his horse, "Jenny, take my bow."

The horse jumped to an immediate gallop. Jenny shot off one arrow. Two Anic arrows missiled past Willard's head. One kicked up dirt inches from the horse's right front hoof.

"Jenny!"

"I know...I know...breath."

Jenny shot off two more. Both missed. However, three of the archers dove for cover. One remained standing. He fumbled with an arrow in his bag. Jenny shot one more. It found its mark in the archer's chest. The other archers remained on the ground.

Jenny said, "Ok, we're clear."

Willard replied, "Now aren't you glad I—"

Jenny replied, "Yes Dad, I'm glad you taught me archery."

Willard smiled.

They easily caught up with the frantic PC. He wasn't an experienced rider. He sat tilted in the saddle and slapped the horse's neck hoping it'd go faster.

"Mr. PC, take it easy on the creature."

The leader of the Enlightened ceased smacking the animal.

"Sir, are you ok?"

Nothing.

Willard galloped a few feet in front of the PC. He looked back at him.

Panic clenched his eyes. Abhorrence cemented into his face.

"Sir, can you hear me?"

Still no response.

Chapter 31

New Avanoor

Fletcher, Longfellow, and Kinton scanned the lines of their neighbors enlisting into New Avanoor's legion for a six month contract.

They were simple farmers, merchants, creators, blacksmiths, protectors, and former legionnaires.

Fletcher said to Kinton, "Correct me if I'm wrong, but I see all of New Avanoor's protectors enlisting. We probably need a few to stay."

Kinton replied, "None of them wanted to. Their wives volunteered."

"Wives?"

"Yes, well, actually wives, sisters, daughters. Our all female protector force is actually double the size of our normal force. And they aren't a happy group of women either."

Fletcher smiled, "Indeed, New Avanoor is probably safer."

Fletcher, Longfellow, and Kinton's heads swiveled to the west. They felt the presence of and heard someone approaching them.

A rugged man in his mid thirties aggressively walked up to Fletcher. He had a full beard, shaggy curly hair, and two black powder weapons slung over his back. He stood well over six feet tall with broad shoulders and a thick chest. He wiped beads of sweat off his forehead.

The stranger asked with a condescending tone, "Are you Chief Fletcher?"

Fletcher carefully said, "Yes, please call me Fletcher."

He looked down to Fletcher and said, "Ahh, the legendary Fletcher. Just an ordinary man. I expected someone seven feet tall, with arms thicker than my legs, and hands stronger than a horse."

Fletcher cautiously looked up at the odd man and asked, "And you are?"

The rugged man held out his hand. Fletcher gripped the stranger's sweaty palm. The bearded man's stiff face morphed into a broad smile.

He said, "Aye, the honor is mine, sir! I know a good man when I see one. I'm Max Lordhunter from the North West Territory. I'm the chief of five hamlets, proud husband of a beautiful wife, a father of three sons, and an owner of four farms and two businesses. I traveled here to see New Avanoor. I wanted to see this city of light with me own eyes. And, of course, to buy Sofia's new invention. How do you pronounce it again? Rufle?"

Fletcher still gripped Max Lordhunter's firm handshake, smiled, and said, "Rifle. And welcome to New Avanoor. Have you fired it yet?"

"Yes, I'm impressed. But I am eager to ask. Is this invasion I hear of true?"

"It is."

Lordhunter nodded and said, "My militia will arrive in three weeks."

Fletcher asked, "Militia?"

"I'm also the general of the North West militia…over two thousand men strong. Half of us were legionnaires in our previous lives before we moved to the land of freedom. We train harder than our days in the legion. Protecting freedom requires strength, diligent elders, and warriors bursting with vehemence. We pioneers of the North West have a surplus of all three."

Fletcher smiled.

Chapter 32

Anic camp outside FC

The king of Anic scanned the smoke filled night horizon. His war advisor sat next to him.

The conqueror said, "I don't know what gave me more satisfaction today…our productive meeting with Bertha and the General or tearing down the PC's grand statue."

Jake poured tea into the King's mug from a gem embedded silver kettle. He stirred sugar into the tea using the PC's personal silver ware. He then served tea to the King's war advisor.

The King's camp remained east of FC atop the hill overlooking the burning city. The fire consuming FC glowed brightly in the dark moonless night. A fresh dusting of gray ash blanketed the smoke enveloped Anic camp.

The advisor brushed ash off his shoulder and replied, "Yes, my majestic king, it was a very productive day."

"But, it's not complete. The PC evaded me."

"Your Excellency, we'll find him. Our legion's best horsemen are on his trail."

The King inquired, "I heard something about a Grasslander bodyguard?"

"Yes sir, three of our archers that watched the PC escape witnessed a Grasslander bodyguard and his young wife protecting the PC."

The King repeated in disbelief, "A Grasslander and his wife as the PC's bodyguards?"

Jake scratched his head.

That's odd.

The advisor said, "Yes almighty king. That was the archers' report."

The King paused.

His lip curled, "Are those archers still alive?"

"No, your majesty. We executed them an hour ago."

The King breathed a sigh of relief.

"Good. It's embarrassing that a female archer forced our men to take cover. And I never want to hear that my legionnaires 'watched' the PC escape again."

"Our generals are aware, sir."

The King stared west towards the burning city. Massive flames engulfing the entire city pumped smoke and soot into the night sky.

The King nodded his head and said, "And who set fire to Federal City? I've spent years dreaming of transforming that city into my personal vacation villa. But, I must confess, I've also dreamt of burning it to the ground."

"Your majesty, we just began the investigation."

"When he's found, I want him burned at the stake…impaled first and then burned. Only I give the order to burn cities."

"Yes, your greatness."

The King added, "I enjoyed tearing down the PC's statue."

The advisor stated, "It didn't fall as I expected. It was awkward how it bent at the feet and flopped down."

"Ha, I thought the same."

Jake glanced around the pitch black camp. The faint hue of the blazing fire ravaging FC provided the only light. Most transgressors were stumbling drunk or busy with FC's women. Three drunks were fighting a few tents away. In the other direction, one warrior stumbled and fell onto a tent. Two occupants crawled out and pummeled the drunk.

Behind Jake, another inebriated Anic rolled off his horse and crashed to the ground. The horse stopped in a dark shadow next to a tree. The rider's body didn't move.

Sacking the capital of the world's most powerful and wealthiest nation had a unique effect on the transgressors' discipline—it vanished.

Slumped on the ground, Jake's personal guard snored. He smelled the mead from the guard's breath. The King and his advisor ignored Jake as they happily fell deep into conversation about the day's bloodshed and destruction.

With an arrowhead, Jake had already cut through the rope binding his feet. Five more minutes and he'd be done with the leash tied to his collar.

Jake kept sawing. He eyed the horse by the tree.

Chapter 33

North of Federal City

The thick rainforest canopy shielded Willard, Jenny, and the PC from the morning sun. The cool air soothed the riders as they trotted along the overgrown trail.

Willard said, "We'll stop for a quick rest."

Jenny tapped her father's shoulder in acknowledgement.

He asked, "How's the PC?"

Jenny looked behind her. The PC was hunched over on the back of the horse's neck. He didn't speak one word the entire night.

"Still sleeping."

"Good."

The trio slowed enough for flies to buzz around their heads. Mosquitoes began nipping at their exposed arms. Willard didn't like the idea of stopping in the middle of the narrow unkempt dirt road. Just the thought made the hair on his neck stand.

The slowing horse woke the PC. After realizing he had slept on a horse he overreacted and instantly gripped the horse's neck out of fear of falling.

Jenny looked back and giggled.

Willard found a small clearing twenty paces off the trail. The hole in the forest was big enough to park three horses.

Willard swung Jenny off the horse. He dismounted.

He said, "Cozy little campground."

Jenny disagreed, "Dad, it's creepy."

"Well, yeah. You've been living the luxurious comfy FC life."

The PC stated, "I agree with your daughter."

Both Willard and Jenny's heads pivoted towards the PC as he carefully slid off his horse.

Willard lightheartedly said, "He speaks!"

The PC didn't smile. He sat on the ground, leaned against a tree, and reached into his bag.

The PC asked, "Why did you save me?"

Willard asked, "What do you mean?"

The PC chewed on a piece of cake.

Jenny knew exactly what he was asking. She remained quiet.

The PC swallowed, "You're a Heartless Grasslander. You people are anti-government. Anti-Enlightenment. Anti-Me. I would expect you to cheer the fall of our capital. Heck, we half expected an army of Heartless to do what Anic just did."

Willard respectfully said, "Sir, that's a myth. The people you call 'Heartless' are the opposite."

"You didn't answer my question. Why did you save me?"

Willard inhaled. He pursed his lips.

"Sir, the Legionnaire Oath expires upon my final breath in this world. You are correct in that I don't agree with many of your policies, but the oath is blind. It cares only for the existence of the Document and what it represents. Sir, a position of leadership is sacred. The Document created the most powerful, and hence, the most sanctified leadership position in the world. I will gladly spill my own blood to protect that…to protect what the Document has created."

Willard turned to Jenny and smiled at her.

He added, "And to protect the future for my posterity."

The PC finished the final piece of cake. He blankly stared at the ground. No words.

Willard turned to his satchel and removed an oat bar. He took a bite.

"I love these things. Your mother makes the best ones, but she changed the ingredients on me again."

Jenny asked, "What changes?"

"The base is the same. Oats, honey, dried blueberries, and ground peanuts. It still tastes great. Maybe she added almonds this—"

The PC interrupted, "Where are we going and what are your plans for me?"

Willard was about to bite down into the oat bar again. He stopped.

"Sir, we're taking you to where it's safe…Avanoor. From there we will defend the Continent."

"How? We have no legions."

"Sir, you underestimate us 'Heartless'."

Willard looked to the south. Through a small break in the dense forest he saw a vertical column of black smoke flowing skyward. The smoke emptied into a massive dark cloud—FC's ashes.

Willard stood and said, "We need to keep moving. The King probably has his best trackers pursuing us."

Astonished, the PC asked, "You said you'd bring me to safety?!"

"I did. We're not there yet."

Chapter 34

New Avanoor

The afternoon sun blazed through the cloudless blue sky. The rare summer humidity of the Northern Territory filled Fletcher's lungs. Sweat trickled off his chin as he stood over a sand pit. Longfellow, Kinton, and Max Lordhunter stood around the pit. Winston laid on his chest in the grass in Fletcher's shadow. He gnawed on a piece of rawhide shaped into a bone.

Fletcher carved a rectangle into the sand and said, "This is the Continent. The King landed in the Southeast. He took the gold mines here. He's most likely at FC by now."

Fletcher drew an "X" and said, "Here's FC. Max, where do you think he'll go next? You've spent time in Anic, right?"

Max replied, "Aye, they are a selfish, corrupt bunch of miscreants. Never trust an Anic. They only care about themselves and won't hesitate to step on their neighbor to better their own life. And they spit on life. They don't value it like we do…pure selfishness. Destroying another human's existence on this planet to add comfort to their own is the norm. Just like the old southern empires our ancestors fought. Fletcher, to answer your question…Avanoor is next."

Kinton said, "But Avanoor has no strategic value. The south has fertile land and the gold mines. There's nothing in the Great Rolling Hills except economically depressed towns."

Max replied, "Protector Kinton, you are correct. But Anics love symbology. The King will take Avanoor."

Fletcher added, "I concur."

Max continued, "And Anics hedge everything. Don't forget about the east and west coasts. He'll hit them with separate forces."

Kinton doubted Max and said, "Jake's note mentioned multiple waves hitting the Southeast. If that's true, he won't have sufficient forces for the other coasts."

Max replied, "Aye, that may be true. Or not."

Max bellowed out a half-crazed laugh.

The group of men stared at the character from the North West.

Longfellow smiled, "I'm glad you're on our side, you crazy nut."

"Ney, I'm on the side of free will."

Fletcher inquired, "Max, why do you think they'll hit the other coasts?"

"Anics don't take a crap without eyeing at least three holes."

Longfellow, Kinton, and Fletcher chuckled knowing they'd never understand. The Anic culture perplexed everyone except for those who lived among them.

Max continued, "Sometimes knowledge can't be acquired from reading a book."

Winston looked up from his rawhide treat. He saw three men nodding and a fourth crazy bearded man smiling. All four men stood around the sand pit. Winston's master held a long branch. The dog's curiosity took control.

He clenched onto his treat and sprang into the sand.

Winston dropped his rawhide bone.

Kinton joked, "Winston, what are your thoughts? Is Avanoor next?"

Winston watched the four men laugh. He wagged his tail. He playfully pushed his rawhide bone over the sand. It rested inside Fletcher's sketch of the Continent.

Longfellow added, "I guess that's a yes!"

Fletcher reached over and drew a circle around Winston's treat and said, "Ok, so Winston's rawhide toy is Avanoor. And he's sitting on New Avanoor. Well, his wagging tail just erased New Avanoor."

Winston stared at the four men smiling down to him. His tongue hung out of his mouth. He lifted his paw into the air and whined.

169

Fletcher shook his head, "Winston, you ate enough already."

Winston shot Fletcher his puppy face. It never worked on Fletcher. He hoped one of the other three men would fall for it.

Nothing.

The men continued staring at Winston. The dog panted in the heat. He slid forward onto his chest. He rested his head onto his front two paws. He poked his sandy rawhide treat with his nose.

Max said, "Aye, Winston, the protector of sheep. I like your idea."

Kinton added, "I was thinking the same thing."

Fletcher concluded, "Defend Avanoor."

Longfellow added, "Then drive those bastards off the Continent."

Max asked, "Aye, but then what?"

Longfellow said, "What do you mean?"

Max said, "That's only the first part. We boot one tyrant out of the Continent for what? So those scoundrels in FC can retake control of the government and screw it up again? Anic will return. They don't rollover and swallow defeat like our Traditionalist politicians. So, I say make Fletcher the PC. Raise massive legions. Build up the navy and invade Anic."

Longfellow and Kinton nodded in agreement. All three looked to the founder of New Avanoor.

Fletcher shook his head, looked directly at Max, and said, "No. We must reinstate Elder Hill and the PC."

Max's eyes widened. Saliva glistened on his lips.

Max shouted, "Are you insane? Those Enlightened are the ones who did this."

Fletcher remained calm and replied, "True, but the Document is sacred. We exist to defend it. Not to tear it up in the name of defending it."

Max vented, "So what do we do? The same PC, the same elders? And don't say 'wait until elections'. We'll replace the old elders with false Traditionalists who will eventually cave to the Enlightened. You are insane for reinstating the same rotten corrupt culture that bankrupted the greatest civilization in history. Politicians are all the same. All they want is power. FC won't change, no matter how many elections. No matter how many new or refreshing candidates we get. They are cut from the same rotten cloth! And when the few goodhearted people do get elected, they are indoctrinated into that putrid culture of Elder Hill. They become one of 'them'. That's indoctrination at its worst. Fletcher, elections get us nowhere. The Traditionalists and Enlightened are the same. They both are the Party of Power. The Party of More Control over Everyone's Life. But by then, Anic will return. With their own improved rifles."

Fletcher calmly replied, "Max, you said earlier that you're on the side of free will. Is it free will for three men to proclaim me as the new PC? Does free will step on the Document that protects free will?"

A slightly calmer Max said, "Sometimes good men must do things they regret to protect free will. I plan to slaughter many Anics."

Fletcher stated, "Killing Anics and defending the Document from those who desire to tear it into shreds is one thing. But nothing justifies us tearing the Document, even in the name of saving it. Spitting on our principles in the name of respecting them is not the way of the great Servius, Crassius, or Kamila."

Max fell silent.

Longfellow agreed with Max Lordhunter and said, "Fletcher, we can't just hand the Continent back to the ones who drove it off a cliff."

Fletcher said, "My father sent messengers across the Continent to not only spread news of the Anic invasion, but to also request Regional Elders to convene in Avanoor."

Max scratched his head, "Why would he do that? We're under invasion. What good are Regional Elders in killing Anics?"

Fletcher replied, "My father requested they travel to Avanoor in hopes of exercising Article Five to amend the Document. It's all about placing more limits and restrictions on the central government's power. For example, one possible amendment to the Document would require more than just a simple majority for tax hikes, borrowing, and increased spending. Maybe a super majority like 3/5 or 3/4 approval. Also, we could create another amendment to simplify cutting taxes and spending. Maybe all that is needed to approve tax and spending cuts is 1/3 of Elder Hill. We can't forget about forbidding Elder Hill from taxing citizens for doing nothing. I'm sure there are Documental legists that can think up more amendment ideas to impede future spending, taxing, and borrowing. Hence, Article Five is our last option."

The men responded with blank stares.

Fletcher asked, "When's the last time any of you actually read the Document?"

The three men shamefully looked down at the ground.

Chapter 35

"Hah….hah!"

Jake dug his heels into the foam covered depleted horse as the sun dropped beneath the trees to his left. He leaned into the corners as the horse galloped around blind turns, over fallen trees, and through puddles. Fresh hoof prints in the mud told the story of what laid ahead.

Jake gripped his bow and squinted in the fading twilight. He felt like he was in a race. Yet, there was no logical reason to ride his horse to near death. Something inside him pushed him. His instincts drove him.

Chapter 36

Willard prodded the weak fire and scattered the embers. Jenny and the PC were already sleeping. Dried mud covered their ragged clothes. The PC used a stone as a pillow.

Willard wouldn't sleep. The Anic warriors weren't far behind. Each night he searched for their smoke column in the moonlight. Each night he found it. The previous night he smelled their dinner.

Willard's inner legionnaire had awoken. He learned long ago how to redirect the immense strength of the human will to survive.

Yet, on this quiet night and despite his heightened state of awareness, he couldn't see anything. The only smell came from the fading embers of the fire.

The breeze came from the south—no smell of Anic dinner.

Willard tightened his bow. He withdrew four arrows and laid them on the ground. The glowing embers succumbed to the pitch black of night. His eyes slowly adjusted to the empty gloom.

Willard scratched his beard. Dirt and grime covered his face, arms, and hands. He smelled days of dried sweat radiating from his mud covered clothes. He chuckled thinking about how the PC attempted to bathe in a mud stream two days earlier. Bathing was futile.

Willard focused on the small entrance to his camp. He purposely chose this location far off the trail. It was hidden, deep into the thick brush, and only had one tight entrance.

Chokepoint.

He hoped the Anics would ride on and miss their hideout. But Willard knew better. The King probably had his best trackers on their tail. No matter how dark and how well he covered their tracks, they would find the two fleeing Grasslanders and their prize passenger.

Willard inhaled deep. He found his rhythm. He exhaled. If there were four Anics, he might have a chance. He could take out two before they knew what hit them.

He closed his eyes and thought of his wife. He thought of his sons—Fletcher and Jake. Pain stabbed his heart. He looked at Jenny's shadowy silhouette. She slept peacefully.

Chapter 37

Fletcher rode his horse into Avanoor. Something wasn't right. It looked different—cleaner and well kept. The city walls were rebuilt taller and thicker. There were more buildings and homes in Avanoor. The road was clean and newly bricked. He barely recognized his home town. He trotted through the main street. Lush tall green trees lined the road.

However, the town was empty.

He approached his parent's home. It looked different. He dismounted and walked to the door. Fletcher stopped.

He heard a voice echo from above.

"Do not fear, my grandson. Be calm. Note carefully all I tell."

Fletcher looked up to the clear blue sky. He saw nothing.

"Grandpa? What's going on?"

"Stay on the path you have chosen. Soon enough it will be your duty to devote to the people the benevolence of your integrity, talent, and wisdom. Be ready; for your country will turn to you and everything you represent. It will be your duty to take on a great burden."

"I don't understand...I—"

"Mark this, for this thought will steel your determination to rush to the defense of your homeland. Every man who has preserved or defended Avanoor and the values that Avanoor represents is reserved a special place with the Divine. Nothing is more pleasing to

Him than the gatherings of men bound together by the oath of right, just, and the responsible exercise of power for the people."

Fletcher continued scanning the skies. He felt a chilly breeze. He looked at the door in front of him.

The voice said, "Enter the door. Step into the place. Do upon the Continent as I have done. Love, justice, and devotion. These are owed both your parents and kinsmen; but more than anything else, they are owed to your country. Go now."

Fletcher gulped and looked down at the handle.

He gripped it and opened the door. A gust of wind blasted Fletcher in the chest. He regained his footing. He gazed into the doorway. He saw the night sky—a place full of stars, shining and splendid. The view was complete and beautiful. He saw stars never seen from the Continent. The smallest of these stars was the one furthest away. Fletcher's eyes focused on that one insignificant sparkle. Somehow he knew that was the sun that rose over Avanoor each day. It was so minute.

Fletcher raised his foot and paused. He felt fear, uncertainty, and vertigo as he stared into the black abyss that gave way to an unceasing pit of the unknown. He also felt an immense burden and strain. Courage filled his soul. He knew what he had to do. For the second time in his life, fate tapped Fletcher Gallatae on the shoulder.

He stepped into the star filled darkness.

He awoke out of the dream. He laid on his back in his bed. He felt pressure on his chest. He blinked. He saw darkness. The stars were no more.

Winston's front paws pressed into Fletcher's rib cage. The dog stared at him—watching him…watching over him.

Chapter 38

Longfellow departed New Avanoor five days earlier; however he made great time as he galloped southeast of New Avanoor. He carried a rifle with him.

He replayed his mission in his mind.

Engage population centers in the eastern Great Rolling Hills and recruit people into New Avanoor's legion. Direct them to rendezvous at Avanoor.

Longfellow figured it'd be relatively easy considering Willard sent out messengers weeks earlier to spread the news of the Anic invasion.

Longfellow had left the Northern Territory and entered the first town under the Continent's jurisdiction. The darkness of night blanketed the grasslands. Exhaustion had gripped Longfellow's eye lids. He would camp here for the night.

Something wasn't right. The moonlight illuminated the absence of activity and people. Longfellow rode into the town center. It was empty. The stores, homes, and public buildings were looted.

Longfellow shook his head.

This place is abandoned.

His eyes focused on one building. Candle light glowed out of the windows and through the crack at the bottom of the door—the town prison.

Longfellow dismounted his horse and unsheathed his sword. He slowly approached the door.

Silence.

He knocked and asked, "Anyone there?"

A voice from inside the jail replied, "Who is asking?"

"I'm Thomas Longfellow and looking for a place to sleep."

The door swung open. A Federal held up his sword. The weasel like stare caught Longfellow off guard. A two week beard grew on the Federal's bony face. His beady eyes sent shivers down Longfellow's spine. The silversmith gripped his sword tighter.

The Federal asked, "What is your business here? Can't you see that everyone has fled?"

"I'm looking for a place to sleep."

The slouching Federal shot back, "Nothing here. Keep traveling."

"May I ask why this place is deserted? Why are you still here?"

The Federal sarcastically laughed and snarled, "Obviously, I have important things to do. You need to think before you speak. And I'm busy right now. Go away."

Longfellow sensed something was awry. He stretched his neck and tried peeking over the weasel's bony shoulder. The Federal shifted his scrawny frame to block Longfellow.

Thomas asked, "Who else is in there with you?"

"None of your business. I'm busy."

Longfellow persisted, "Who else?"

He heard a muffled voice moan in the back.

Longfellow asked, "Who's that?"

The Federal replied by slamming the door in Longfellow's face. The candle light flashed into darkness.

Longfellow ran to the back of the prison. He shook the door. *Locked.*

Those beady eyes had burned into Longfellow's mind.

I have to get in there.

He returned to the front of the building, jumped onto his horse, and approached the front door. He turned the creature around and backed into the door.

He spoke to his horse, "Alright boy, I need you to kick your hind legs back and bust that door down."

The horse nodded his head as if he understood Longfellow. The horse kicked the door off the hinges. He heard a feminine scream.

Longfellow dismounted and rushed into the prison with his sword at the ready. He jumped onto the collapsed door. It had pinned the whimpering Federal to the ground. Longfellow pointed his sword inches from the pathetic man's cowardly face.

"What's going on here?"

The miscreant begged, "Please...please, don't hurt me...I...I—"

Longfellow shifted more weight onto the door. The weasel shrieked. Longfellow heard the muffled voice from the back of the prison again.

"Who is back there?"

More moans.

Longfellow punched the miscreant in the head, shoved the heavy door, and dragged the bony Federal to a chair. He tied his hands and feet to it. He found the candle and lit it. He wiped sweat from his palms and the hilt of his sword as he cautiously stepped to the back of the prison.

He heard more muffled groans and saw a figure slumped on the ground.

Longfellow unlocked the jail cell and removed the prisoner's gag.

The prisoner said, "Thank the Divine!"

Longfellow asked, "What's going on here?"

"That spineless lowlife arrested me."

Longfellow asked, "I...I think I met you in Avanoor. You are one of Willard's messengers?"

"Thank the Divine again!"

"Why are you locked up?"

"That scum arrested me because I had a horse. Then he learned of Willard's message."

He unbound the prisoner's hands and feet.

Longfellow asked, "Why are both of you still in this deserted town?"

"I'm his prize. He thinks I'm part of some grand conspiracy to overthrow the Enlightened. He thinks Willard is coordinating with the invading horde to the east."

"Invading horde to the east?!"

"I guess the news hasn't made it to Avanoor yet. The invaders to the east aren't Anic. That's why this town is empty. Everyone fled south. There was nothing I could do. The Federal had me in here."

In disbelief, Longfellow said, "No…it can't be."

"It's true. And these townspeople are fleeing right into the Anics."

Longfellow's mind raced. This wasn't the first time he heard about an invasion on the eastern coast.

Max Lordhunter was right.

Longfellow said, "The guys in New Avanoor half expected them to hit the east coast. They probably are on our west coast too. Now what's with this Federal's 'grand conspiracy'?"

"I don't know. Don't try and reason with that imbecile. That man's brain is warped. It doesn't function right. He's a deceitful scumbag too. He tries to impress people with his knowledge of FC legal code. He's condescending, talks down to everyone, and doesn't hesitate to yield his power if someone dares question his knowledge and authority. He even treats the town chief and elders like the bottom of a craphole."

"But still, why is he holding you here instead of fleeing?"

The prisoner continued venting, "Don't be fooled by this fraud. His personal agenda drives him. You'd think he's Anic in how he doesn't flinch to tear others down for his own gain. He's a spineless shark—"

"Hey, you can vent later. Why are both of you still here?"

The prisoner replied, "I told you, personal agenda. He convinced himself of this grand conspiracy and is 'waiting' for more Federals to arrive, take me away, and reward him for cracking the conspiracy. Nothing drives a man crazier than listening to a crazy man hold a conversation with himself about what he plans to do with his new fame and wealth. He wants to write a book, create a National Conspiracy Force to exterminate the Heartless, and forever silence Hudson."

Longfellow said, "No wonder why we are bankrupt and under invasion."

"Yeah, it's torture just being in the same room with the guy. You know that chilly feeling you get when a snake slivers by your feet? Yeah, imagine that feeling, but all day long."

"I noticed that. Just listening to his voice and seeing those beady eyes made me nauseous."

"The guy even hisses like a snake."

Longfellow said, "Alright, alright, enough wasting good oxygen talking about this unfortunate creature. Let's get you out of here, eat some grub, and find a place to sleep."

"What about the snake?"

Longfellow chuckled, "He's fine where he's at now. We'll untie him in the morning before we leave."

Chapter 39

Willard fought his eyelids. They wanted to close but his will power wouldn't let them. Willard glanced over at his sleeping daughter. That's all he needed to remain alert.

The veil of darkness covering the camp dissolved. Rays of bright moonlight shot through a break in the clouds and trees. The clean light painted his camp in shades of feint blue-gray.

Something was near. He couldn't hear it. He felt no rumbling of horses in the distance. But he knew something was approaching. Willard instinctively gripped his bow with his left hand. His right hand fell onto an arrow. He waited. His thoughts drifted to his home. He warmed thinking of his wife. He pondered what crops to plant for the following year. His house needed renovations too. His "chore list" rolled through his mind.

I may not have to worry about any of that.

He could feel the rumbling.

Willard's mind raced.

How many horses?

They were too far to estimate.

The camp still glowed in the fresh moonlight. However, Willard kneeled under the canopy of a tree. Blackness swallowed Avanoor's head protector.

The rumbling of galloping horses grew louder. Willard cursed.

At least six horses...too many.

Willard gripped a second arrow. He'd double shoot. He hasn't shot double in over a decade. It was risky. It was his only option.

He still hoped for the slim possibility they would gallop by his cozy hidden campground.

They didn't.

The rumbling slowed to a light trot. He heard voices. It was the Anic tongue.

Willard's heart pounded the inside of his chest. His eyes focused on the entrance. He pulled the two arrows back on the bow.

Any second.

Images of his wife calmed Willard's nerves. He pictured her peaceful face. Willard smiled. The trembling in his hands ceased.

Please God, let me live this day.

The first Anic emerged from the dark forest and stepped into the moonlit camp—sword drawn. His long braided hair hung down to his shoulders. His thick beard, cold white eyes, and sleeveless shirt displayed the warrior's strength. The massive Anic scanned the camp. His eyes found Jenny and the PC. A second Anic, bald but with thicker arms covered in tattoos, slowly materialized out of the darkness. The first Anic held two fingers up and whispered to the bald one. They were standing inches from each other.

Willard released the double shot.

Swoosh. Thump, thump.

The braided Anic caught the arrow in his neck and collapsed to the ground. Without flinching, the bald Anic ripped the other arrow out of his own shoulder. He charged Willard's hiding spot and screamed in his Anic tongue. Three more Anics poured into the campground behind the bald crazed warrior.

The head protector gripped one more arrow and pulled back on his bow.

Swoosh.

The third arrow found its mark—the Anic's heart. The bald madman gripped the arrow. His eyes rolled to the back of his head and his body crashed to the ground.

Willard jumped to his feet as he watched the three new Anics charge.

Still hidden in the shadow, he readied two more arrows. He pulled back on the bow. His peripheral vision observed five more Anics flooding into the campground.

184

Willard cursed in his head.

Kill eight more…or never see my wife and children again.

He released the double shot. One arrow missed. The other one pierced into an Anic's stomach. All three continued to charge.

Still invisible to the Anics, Willard stepped to the side. He unsheathed his sword and ducked behind a bush. The three Anics entered Willard's pitch black world untouched by moonlight. They found nothing.

Willard sprang out from the bush and struck two Anics. The cool sharp Avanoorean steel sliced into their flesh and pierced their hearts.

Six more to kill.

Two Anics tied Jenny and the PC's ankles. The other three took up security around the two Anics and their prizes.

Jenny screamed.

The Anic with an arrow still lodged in his stomach watched his two comrades fall to Willard's sword. He caught Willard distracted as his daughter screamed. Willard's sharpened reflexes and bloodied sword deflected the incoming Anic steel, but he lost his balance and his weapon. The Anic pummeled Willard's face with his massive fist. The Avanoorean fell onto his back and into the moonlight.

He looked up as the Anic thrusted his sword inches from Willard's face.

Another Anic yelled, "I want that scum alive."

The Anic hovering over Willard reluctantly obeyed his boss.

Two more Anics stepped towards the defenseless Avanoorean.

The lead Anic shook his head and said, "Futile. I don't understand why you think you could outrun us. But I am impressed you killed four of my men. You must be a true legionnaire, not one of those spineless worms of FC."

Willard cursed the Anic. He had to buy time.

He said, "You don't know what you're up against. Leave us alone and we will let you live."

The Anics laughed.

The lead Anic said, "You might be one of the few true warriors of the old legions, but you're dumber than those clueless federal elders. They squealed like pigs as we slit their throats."

Willard replied, "This land is divine. Leave us now."

The Anic grew frustrated, "You stubborn goat. The king of Anic is the Divine. This is now his land."

He pointed down at Willard and said, "Kill this insolent—"

Swoosh.

An arrow shot into the lead Anic's head. The tip of the arrow protruded out of his forehead. Hair and bits of brain on the arrowhead glistened in the moonlight. Blood streamed down his face and off his chin. His eyes crossed. The Anic fell forward.

Swoosh, swoosh.

Two more Anics fell with arrows lodged in their backs.

A voice yelled, "Get up old man!"

Willard shot to his feet. That voice was familiar—an Avanoorean dialect.

The stranger and Willard charged the three remaining Anics standing by Jenny and the PC. The PC and his tea girl were lying on the ground with bounded ankles. Jenny's hands were still untied. She stabbed her dagger into an Anic's calves and the back of his knees. He screamed and slumped onto the ground next to her. She slit his throat.

The sound of swords slicing through neck and bone echoed through the moonlit camp. Blood splattered onto Jenny's face and arms while she watched one Anic head bounce onto the ground next to her. A second head landed on the PC's stomach. Freshly sprayed with Anic blood, he felt the head's fractured spinal bone poke him in the gut. The head's deathly stare hooked the PC's eyes. The elected leader of the Continent shrieked as Willard kicked the Anic head off his stomach. The PC vomited.

The underworld awaited all ten Anics.

The bearded stranger turned to Willard and squinted in the faint moonlight.

Willard said, "Thank the Divine. You saved—"

The stranger replied in shock, "Dad?"

Chapter 40

The king of Anic strolled through the smoldering ashes of FC. He walked with his hands behind his lower back. He slept less as each night passed without word from his ten man squad sent to retrieve the PC. He passed time by rummaging through the destroyed metropolis growing angrier by the day that the PC had evaded him.

The King stepped over a smoldering body, turned to his military advisor, and said, "Remind me on why must we wait here again."

"Your majesty, the gold. We haven't found FC's gold yet."

"Yes, yes. The gold. I think less of gold and more of my destiny. I want my throne in Avanoor. And that PC's head impaled on an Anic spear and forever placed at the entrance to Avanoor."

"Yes my lord, yes, but we must have gold to pay our legion. We bypassed the gold mines, the gem filled rivers, and the diamond hills in the Southeast. The follow on waves of our Anic brethren will reap that reward. The plundering in this ashen city has been insufficient. We must find the gold."

The King coldly stated, "There are no follow on waves hitting the Southeast."

The advisor asked, "What? My most majestic King, please forgive my questions, but—"

"I lied to you all. I sent the other Anic legions to meet with the invasion forces of the kingdoms across the East and West Seas. No other Anic is allowed to touch the Southeast. These men who stand here with us today will have years to plunder the hills and rivers in the Southeast. And I will grant land ownership to any man from this legion who desires to mine, farm, and raise Anic families."

The advisor understood and said, "Your divine cleverness outwits even your wisest advisor. I understand the ruse now. You must have sent members of our legion to purposely surrender and spread misinformation about the follow on waves."

The King nodded, "You are correct. And only you shall hear these next words. After colonizing our share of the Continent and building more legions, we will invade the remainder of the Continent from the other kingdoms. As they weaken their home defenses by shipping their legions across the seas to the Continent to fight us, Anic will invade and strike the hearts of their kingdoms."

"Yes, yes almighty King. The entire world will bow to you soon. That is your destiny."

The King said, "But I digress. Tell our fine warriors this…tell them that no other Anic is allowed to step one foot in the Southeast. That is their land. That is their plunder. But we will not return to the Southeast just yet."

The advisor nodded and said, "Yes, the great king of Anic. The men will be happy to hear this news."

The King added, "And stop looking for wealth in this city of ashes. There is no gold here. The Continent is broke. Their wealth was nothing more than rotten paper notes containing empty promises."

The advisor bowed and said, "Yes, your highness."

The King said, "It'll take a full cycle of the moon for my legion to recover from their hangovers, pack, and march to Avanoor."

The advisor bowed, turned, and briskly walked away. The King stopped walking. He looked up at the one remaining structure in FC completely untouched by the fire. The unblemished white marble monument contrasted with the blackened ruins of FC.

The statue of Crassius.

The King kneeled at the foot of the historic statue. He stared up at Crassius and then bowed his head. A tear rolled down the King's cheek.

Chapter 41

Willard asked, "When are you going to shave that beard?"

Jake replied, "I'm somewhat liking it."

Jenny added, "You'll give mother a heart-attack."

Jake smirked, "We could bound my hands and put a leash around my neck before we return home. Play a joke on—"

Willard chuckled and said, "I'm glad to see that the Anics succeeded at only corrupting your sense of humor."

The PC slept on the back of his horse again as the party of four headed north.

The three Avanooreans and their one guest were only a few days out from Avanoor. Their spirits were high. They ached for a bath and then a soaking in Avanoor's hot spring. They yearned for a clean set of clothes to cover their sore bodies.

The cool summer weather welcomed them as they traveled further north into the Great Rolling Hills. The refreshing breeze from the north and the comfort of being surrounded by grasslands welcomed the travelers.

Jake asked, "So, Jenny, how was your residency?"

Willard warned, "I wouldn't go there."

Jenny chuckled, "Yeah, please don't. Hopefully, years from now I'll look back and laugh at that experience. I gave up trying to understand FC during my second week there after I learned that prayer and the national flag were prohibited from schools. Flags were unsafe and prayer violated the separation of church and state.

However, history lessons of the Enlightened and the infallibility of their policies were mandatory for each grade."

Jake added, "Well, I wouldn't let Federal City bother you anymore. The entire city has burnt to ashes. Everything is gone…flattened."

Willard replied, "I'm shocked that the King would destroy the city. I figured he'd want to make it a resort. I'll give the Enlightened credit on one thing, they have a gift for creating luxury and excess."

Jake replied, "You're right Dad, the King wasn't happy watching it burn."

The three Avanooreans and the PC arrived at a crossroads in the open plains. A party of Regional Elders and protectors approached from the west. Five protectors galloped ahead and approached the ragged looking group coming from the south.

A protector firmly asked, "Who are you?"

Willard answered, "I'm Head Protector Willard Gallatae of Avanoor. Who is asking?"

A gray haired, red faced Regional Elder overheard Willard's reply. A smile shot across his face as he trotted towards the crossroads behind the five protectors.

The protector replied cautiously, "We are providing escort to the Regional Elders behind us. If you are the head protector of Avanoor, what is your business coming from the south?"

Willard didn't answer. He focused on the gray haired elder approaching from behind the five protectors. He looked familiar.

The old man rode in front of the protectors and said, "Willard!"

Willard's eyes lit up, "Elder Cicero! My brother in arms!"

The two men dismounted from their horses and embraced. Willard and Cicero stepped back and vigorously shook hands.

"My Divine, how many years has it been? Eight?"

Willard replied, "Eight or nine. Either way, it's been too long my old friend."

"And it smells like you haven't bathed for nine years either!"

Willard replied, "It's been a long couple weeks."

Cicero said, "You must tell. But first let's make camp, cook some of our finest foods and celebrate."

Cicero turned to his five protectors and said, "Break out the fine wine tonight!!"

A protector replied, "But Elder Cicero, you said that the wine should be reserved for the first night at Avanoor."

Cicero replied, "Yes, the first night at Avanoor with my good friend Willard. Break out the wine tonight, my young man!"

The protector nodded.

Willard said, "You haven't changed one bit, have you!"

"I age like wine, my good friend. But I much prefer drinking it."

The two men embraced again.

Cicero added, "And brother, your message has awoken a sleeping giant."

Chapter 42

New Avanoor

"The sun never shined on a cause of greater worth."-Thomas Paine

Fletcher hugged Sofia. He kissed her cheek.

"Sofia, keep those rifles coming."

Sofia choked up, "Of course I will."

She forced a smile. Fletcher turned around. He walked towards the thousands of New Avanoorean legionnaires sitting on their horses in formation. Fletcher wore full leather armor, an engraved breastplate, and his old legionnaire uniform. His sheathed sword hung from his belt. He held his helmet in his left hand.

Sofia couldn't hold back anymore. Tears streamed down her cheeks. She shut her eyes and wiped the drops off her chin.

Fletcher arrived at his horse in the front of the legion. Gust, Kinton, and Max Lordhunter waited for him.

Max smiled, "You like her? Aye?"

Fletcher avoided the question and said, "We should be going now. It's half a moon to Avanoor."

A cool late summer breeze blew from the north. Clouds blocked the afternoon sun.

Fletcher nodded at Gust. He nodded back and lifted up a large green flag and waved it. The four leaders heard the company commanders behind them giving the order to move forward. The New Avanoor legion headed south. Fletcher turned to his right. The loyal Winston looked up at the New Avanoor's chief. Fletcher smiled at his friend and four legged protector.

Chapter 43

"A nation's true source of wealth is the divine flame in each human spirit. A truly great society frees and protects that boundless energy." – Old John

Jake stood and departed the group of young protectors and Jenny. He held his full stomach as he walked through the dark night towards the campfire surrounded by Cicero, his father, and the other Regional Elders. He felt awkward watching two of the protectors flirt with his sister. It was time to join the old men.

Cicero watched Jake walk towards the group. The Regional Elder gulped down his fifth goblet of wine.

He stood and said, "Young Jake! Your father told me of what you've endured these last few months. I must say, we each lived through similar situations."

Willard and the other elders nodded.

Elder Cicero held out his hand and said, "Others over self. Welcome to the brotherhood."

Each intoxicated elder stood, shook hands, and embraced Jake. Willard was the last to hug his son.

He said, "Son, you are a true Gallatae. And I'm a proud father. Your grandfather and our ancestors are smiling down on you."

Jake humbly lowered his head.

Willard continued, "Son, the Continent grew strong not solely because of natural resources, fertile land, and the Document. Pure

194

hearted men of integrity like you and my fellow brothers sitting around this campfire enabled the Continent to prosper."

Cicero picked up a flask of wine and recharged everyone's goblet.

He said, "I will make a toast."

The elders and Willard all said, "Aye."

Cicero continued, "To the Divine for protecting these great men. I am honored and humbled that you call me 'brother'."

The men raised their goblets and said, "To the Divine."

Cicero continued, "Now young Jake, how much did you study about Natural Law and the divinity of human spirits?"

Willard and the elders caught eyes and joked, "Ahhh, there goes Cicero the drunken philosopher again."

Jake replied, "Only what we studied at school, but to be candid, it wasn't my favorite subject."

Cicero chuckled, "Understandable. I wasn't much interested in philosophy when in school either."

After sipping his wine, Jake said, "Well, you got me a little more interested."

Cicero said, "Well, good. So, simply put, Natural Law comes from the Divine."

Jake asked, "I have a question. If so, how did we mere mortals learn of it?"

"Hold on there young Jake! We must think this out rather than jump to the end."

Jake nodded.

Cicero continued, "Natural Law is deeply engrained in the human spirit. How so you may ask? The Divine created humans and endowed us mere mortals with a bit of His own divinity."

Jake added, "My days in philosophy class are coming back to me now. That's why we humans have the powers of speech, reason, and thought."

"Yes, yes. Healer School didn't erase all the philosophy that you learned. Now, due to this spark of divinity inside each human, we must be related to the Divine in some fashion. Jake, what can you ascertain from knowing that we share reason with the Divine?"

Jake replied, "Well, the Divine is benevolent. If we share reason with Him and if we humans employ reasoning correctly, then we are also benevolent."

"Yes! Indeed we are! Hence, Natural Law is simply whatever promotes benevolence and forbids evil. How do we translate Natural Law into Natural Rights?"

No one answered.

Cicero said, "Ok, someone name infractions of Natural Law."

Jake stated, "Taking another human's life and stealing from another person."

"Great, but there is one more—oppression. Why does man labor his entire life?"

Jake answered, "He wants to better the lives of his family. He's pursuing happiness."

"And oppression is a violation of the right to pursue happiness. Hence, infractions of Natural Law are infringements on Natural Rights. That's how we get the right to life, liberty, and the pursuit of happiness. Ok, young Jake. Are you ready to move on?

The healer nodded.

Cicero asked, "What did Servius create?"

"Well, he enforced Natural Rights."

"Yes, but more than that. Servius didn't exactly enforce Natural Rights. Avanoor's culture at the time already did that. Servius merely wrote it down and created the foundation for a future society to be built on protecting our Natural Rights."

Jake answered, "Servius created the Document to protect our life, liberty, and the pursuit of happiness."

Willard jumped into the conversation, "You got it. When a human no longer has to focus his energy on protecting his life, liberty, and property, he is freed. His energy is freed. His energy can be redirected to improving his life and his family's lives—the pursuit of happiness. He can build more, create more, and own more. He can pursue entrepreneurial endeavors knowing that his life, liberty, and his creations are protected by the Document. No other society in the world protects such freedom."

Cicero sipped his wine and added, "That's the definition of freedom—unbounded use of your divine energy. A free man doesn't need to expend his energy to protect his life and liberty. Unfortunately, people…like our friend sleeping over there…distorted the true definitions of freedom and rights."

Cicero pointed to the PC sleeping on the other side of the horses.

He continued, "They redefined freedom and rights as something the government gives to people—the right to a job, the right to a home, and the right to eat."

Jake added, "And the government had to borrow vast amounts of money from other kingdoms to pay for these man-made rights."

Willard said, "And don't forget about the quantitative easing and taxes over the last decade. Man is not free if the government takes over half of his income and then uses that money to prevent him from starting a business or innovating—pursuing happiness. And only the misguided believe that fundamental economic growth comes from manipulating currencies and stimulus spending. True economic growth comes from the sweat of entrepreneurs and small business owners. Certain monetary decisions and stimulus spending—in the name of helping the economy—actually devalued our currency, fueled inflation, and impaired the real engine of economic growth."

Cicero added, "Yes, the infamous 'War on the Rich' and the false belief that monetary artifice grows the economy."

Willard said, "The role of government is to protect Natural Rights. The people made a social contract with those they trusted with power to protect their rights, their freedom, and to provide conflict resolution. And they should pay the minimal amount of taxes to fund that protection."

Cicero added, "That's exactly what Servius did. He wrote a social contract that protected our freedom. He formalized Avanoor's justice system to follow something called 'Equal Justice Under Law'. And this freedom and blind justice unlocked the divine energy in the human spirit to fuel the pursuit of a better life."

Jake concluded, "So, in summary, what Servius created—the Document—unleashed mankind's divine energy and stifled evil?"

Cicero replied, "Indeed, my young brother, indeed."

Chapter 44

"If ever a Time should come, when vain and aspiring men shall possess the highest seats in Government, our country will stand in need of its experienced patriots to prevent its ruin." –Samuel Adams

Longfellow and the messenger continued east. They arrived in the largest population center of their trip. The bright moon in the cloudless sky illuminated the town. They rode towards the town center and entered into a cloud of confused energy. Longfellow smelled fear. He sensed panic in the people hurrying through the streets towards the town hall.

The two riders dismounted their horses as people streamed into the meeting place. Anxiety poured out of the door.

Longfellow grabbed the arm of one man bustling towards the entrance.

"Excuse me sir, but what's going on?"

The stranger shot Longfellow a bewildered look and asked, "You haven't heard?"

Longfellow replied, "I just arrived in town."

"We're holding a final meeting to discuss where to go and what to do. We keep having meetings but doing nothing. Many other towns have already fled."

Longfellow released the stranger's arm. The frustrated man disappeared into the town hall. The door slammed shut. Another person darted past the two travelers, cracked the door open, and slid in. The door creaked shut.

Longfellow said, "Stay out here and watch the horses."

The messenger nodded.

Longfellow stepped into the dimly lit town hall and squeezed his way into the anxious, but silent crowd. In the front he saw the head protector facing the crowd.

The protector held his hand up and said, "My friends and neighbors."

He paused and glanced around the packed hall. Silence filled the air.

"The Eastern Mountains are two weeks away. With resistance, King Zevack's forces will arrive in a month. Our town is on the road to FC. Hence, we must act now. We must stop talking and prepare—"

A man's shaky voice interrupted, "Prepare for what? Our deaths? No legions stand between them and our homes."

The crowd murmured. Panic echoed off the walls.

The protector firmly said, "Everyone, calm down. Please calm down. That's why we are here tonight…to finalize our plan."

The hall fell silent again.

He continued, "As we concluded last night, remaining in our homes is not an option. Heading north as the winter's freeze blankets the Continent is not one either. With the exception of those who have relatives to the north, it is recommended we seek shelter in the south. We start packing in the morning. Take only what you can carry on your backs."

Longfellow shook his head.

They don't know about the Anics…just like every other town that didn't get Willard's message.

The protector continued, "The only other option is to head southwest. The traveling will be longer and we must avoid FC. We've concluded that the horde to the east is aiming for FC. Hence, they'll be following our path. We also risk the dangers of an early winter catching us as we travel."

The silversmith had enough.

He bellowed from the back of the hall, "You can't go south or southwest."

All heads turned. Eye's landed on him. The stare of hundreds of frightened and confused townspeople sent shivers down his spine.

Longfellow continued, "The Anics. The Anics have already or are about to take FC. Traveling south will mean certain death or slavery."

Panic erupted from the crowd. The head protector yelled for everyone to calm.

He asked, "Stranger and bringer of sour news, please identify yourself."

Longfellow inhaled and said, "I am Thomas Longfellow, son of the great silversmith from the south. The very south you intend on fleeing to. I escaped days before my home was struck by the Anics."

The protector replied, "We've heard no such news. How can we trust you?"

Longfellow addressed the crowd, "Who here knows Anic? Knows of their language or weapons?"

The crowd murmured again. One man in the middle of the bustle raised his hand.

"I know of Anic."

Longfellow asked, "Could you come here, please?"

The man sucked in his chest and squeezed through the standing crowd. As he neared the back Longfellow held out the bloodied Anic arrow.

The man gripped the Anic weaponry and scrutinized it.

He nodded, "This is indeed an Anic arrow."

Another man yelled out, "I saw this stranger ride in from the northwest with a friend. If you truly escaped from the south, why did you come from—"

Longfellow interrupted the stranger, "I delivered a note from Protector Willard to New Avanoor. That's where I came from."

The head protector nodded and asked, "May I ask what my good friend Willard has planned? We have no legions. No defense. Fleeing is our only option."

Longfellow addressed the crowd again, "Who here is a former legionnaire?"

A third of the people in the hall raised their hands. The head protector scanned the multitude of former warriors. He nodded and smiled.

Longfellow said, "That's what Willard has planned."

Chapter 45

"Liberty and freedom are so very precious that you do not fight and win them once and stop. They are prizes awarded only to those peoples who fight to win them and then keep fighting eternally to hold them!" -Sergeant York

Guardians of God's Gift

The embers in the campfire faded. Cicero emptied the final drops of wine into everyone's goblets.

Cicero slurred, "That's the last of it."

Willard added, "Good drink, my friend."

Cicero smiled, "I only consume the best spirits."

Willard burped, "Now, where were we?"

Jake replied, "The purpose of government."

Cicero said, "Yes, yes. Governments don't make society better. Governments don't increase the standard of living. Governments don't create jobs. And governments don't provide happiness. What governments should do is protect a man's life, liberty, and property so he can focus his energy on pursuing happiness and improving the lives of his family members. That is freedom. And freedom allows the flame of an individual's divine energy to burn brightly. When the people strive to improve the lives of their posterity then society as a whole advances. That flame of benevolence inside each of us is a powerful force."

Cicero sipped his final goblet of wine. One elder gently snored. Another slowly drifted to sleep.

Cicero continued, "The Divine created each human. He has touched each of us with His energy. That makes humans capable of divine acts. It is the human's choice to use that energy to invent and discover. Hence, the Divine speaks through us by innovation. By ideas. By reason."

Willard said, "Servius knew. He knew the power of God's gift in each of us. All it needed was a fertile ground. The Document laid the foundation for that free and fertile environment for the divinity in humans to come to fruition."

Jake asked, "So, God's gift is the divine flame inside each of us?"

Both Willard and Cicero nodded.

Cicero stated, "Jake, your father said something important earlier tonight. He said that the Continent grew strong not only because of our natural resources, but because of pure hearted men like you."

Jake humbly nodded.

Cicero continued, "The Document, this society, and Natural Law mean nothing without the guardians of God's gift. Our society would collapse without men like you to protect the divine flame in each human, enforce the Document, and fight evil."

Willard added, "Malice is the plague of society. We must protect our brethren from evil spirits who prowl about the world seeking the ruin of souls."

Cicero praised, "Well put Willard. Evil will always exist. We can never defeat it. All that we can do is repeatedly beat it down and relentlessly kick it in the corner."

Cicero held his empty goblet over his mouth. A final few drops fell onto his tongue.

He looked at Jake and said, "The Continent might be bankrupt and under invasion. It may appear our great society has plummeted off a cliff and into the history books. Fear not young Jake. This is only the natural cycle of evil attempting to bring down what is good. And it's happened to each generation."

Cicero fell silent. He glanced around at his audience. A third elder had fallen asleep.

He continued, "Ok, well, this cycle of evil is a bit more extreme than usual. But each generation since Servius has stood up, repelled evil, and passed the Continent onto their children."

Willard added, "Jake, just like Cicero and my other brothers around this campfire tonight, you are and will always be a guardian of God's gift. We will succeed. We will defeat the Anics and the kingdoms from across the West and East Seas. Our brotherhood of guardians is strong."

Jake looked into his half empty goblet of wine. His spirit was partially lifted. However, he was enslaved by the Anics for most of the summer. He knew what Avanoor was up against. He watched Arlo and the Commander capitulate without even a thought.

Jake gulped down the remaining wine. He thought it'd be best to keep his final thought to himself.

Without Divine intervention, the King is right. The Continent will be nothing more than an obscure side note in history.

Cicero's eyes focused on Jake.

The Regional Elder said, "Have faith that the Divine will bring good things out of what has happened. It is his specialty."

Willard concluded, "And God causes all things to work together for good as long as those who are called according to His purpose freely choose to guard His gift."

Chapter 46

Avanoor - one month later

The rumbling of the earth shook the Avanooreans sheltering inside the earthen walls of the town hall. Mothers gripped their children. Old John attempted to soothe the anxiety by telling stories of Avanoor's history. One young boy headed to the exit. He peaked outside. His jaw dropped. His eyes widened.

Fletcher, Max, Gust, Longfellow, and Kinton rode their horses past the town hall. Fletcher saw the boy stealing a peak. The chief of New Avanoor smiled. The boy froze in awe.

The older brother found his younger sibling watching the legionnaires.

He said, "That's the sight of freedom."

The young boy looked back and said, "I want to be a legionnaire when I grow up."

He smiled, "Little brother, we both will."

The two brothers slid out of the town hall and watched thousands of legionnaires flow through Avanoor. The thunder of tens of thousands of hooves pounding the earth sent shivers through their spines. The two children were in awe at what they witnessed.

Old John walked outside and stood next to the children. He watched the legionnaires, wielding their rifles, ride past.

He said, "What Federal City stifled is the very thing that will save the Continent."

The clouds blocked the morning's fresh sunlight. The legion formed outside Avanoor's southern wall. The Anic army was visible in the distant horizon to the south.

Fletcher scanned the thousands of legionnaires sitting atop their horses. He could see more than the heat of their lungs in the chilly fall morning. He felt the energy radiating from his brethren. The determination in their eyes fueled Fletcher. The men cheered for him to speak.

But I despise speaking.

He cleared his mind, filled his lungs with the crisp fall air, and spoke from his heart.

"We wouldn't be here on the brink of war, possibly inhaling our final breaths of life, if our families were not threatened by the invading Anics. However, there is more than that reason. Like Servius and Crassius, we carry the tools of death not for conquest, not for power, and not for glory. We wield them for our posterity.

"We cannot let the Continent crumble into the history books. We will rid our land of those who seek violence and who desire to destroy what makes us human. The greatest treasure that a man can hand to his children is a country that protects the people and their God given rights. That is why we stand here today."

Fletcher watched his simple words ignite the legion. Hundreds of heads nodded.

Max said, "Aye, Fletcher, aye."

Fletcher inhaled. The men yearned to hear more of his words.

The leader of New Avanoor continued, "We are here to protect the gift of divine energy that God has given each human. That is what it means to fight for freedom. For liberty. There is no greater honor befallen to man."

I talk too much. Need to close out.

"Over 240 years ago, in this very spot we stand today, the great Servius said 'Never again. Never again will evil strike Avanoor.' This is where Servius led forty-three men into the first battle against the savages. My brothers, we stand here today for the same reason— to safeguard our nation from extinction!"

Fletcher scanned the thousands of brave souls who joined him on the precipice of war. Each horse wore a yellow sheet, covering their chests, stitched with a black LF. Longfellow's storied flag proudly displayed the white LF. Max Lordhunter's flag was different from all others. Four words were stitched into the red and white fabric.

DON'T TREAD ON ME.

Fletcher turned to Max and said, "I'm not much of a speaker."

Max chuckled, "Aye, I could have told you that."

Fletcher smiled, "Thanks, brother."

In a serious tone, Max stated, "Fletcher, this is God's will."

"How so?"

"The day I met you and learned of the invasion is when I realized my purpose. Each major event in my life built up to that day. It wasn't luck. It wasn't coincidence. I pursued what I felt was right and those decisions led me here. It's divine providence. My purpose in life is for this day. This fight."

Lordhunter pointed south to the Anic warriors on the horizon and said, "And to kill them."

Fletcher smiled and rested his hand on Lordhunter's shoulder.

He said, "Max, it's more than today. It's more than just stopping Anic. This is only the beginning."

"Aye, I can feel it too. My blood speaks to me."

Fletcher said, "Max, you know, I've always wanted to ask you something."

"Aye, go ahead, brother."

"What is your bloodline?"

Lordhunter smiled, looked to the south, and nodded, "Aye, my bloodline is one of creators, healers, and legionnaires. It's one of modesty and honor."

Lordhunter turned and faced Fletcher.

He said, "I have the blood of Merci in my veins."

Fletcher replied, "Merci Benevulus? The legendary Merci...prisoner of the southern empires?"

"Aye."

Fletcher stated, "She only had one child...conceived by the—"

"Aye, the emperor's child. I guess my sister didn't tell you."

"Who is your sister?"

"Sofia Lordhunter."

Astounded, Fletcher stuttered, "Your sister?! But...her last name isn't...why didn't you tell me?"

Max said, "She kept our mother's maiden name while she was a surveyor. Lordhunters aren't welcome in Federal City."

Fletcher smiled.

Lordhunter rested his hand on Fletcher's shoulder and added, "Now let's use that divine energy you keep talking about to spill some Anic blood."

Light snow began drifting from the sky. The sun peeked through a small crack in the thick clouds and glinted off Sofia's invention. Fletcher's hand fell onto his rifle. He gripped the cold barrel.

There will be much death today, but not for my men.

He slid his hand back to his sword. He felt the cold scabbard. Fletcher gripped the hilt and withdrew Servius's sword out of its sheath. He lifted the historic weapon over his head.

Freedom wasn't the only treasure Servius handed down to his posterity.

The roar of thousands of men erupted behind him. The ground thundered. The Avanoorean relic sent a shockwave of energy through the legion.

Fletcher focused on the invading Anic army on the horizon. He took a deep breath. He held his sword out in front and dug his heels into the horse. He gripped the saddle as the creature jumped forward. Light snow began flying into his face. His eyes watered from the cold air stinging his eyes. He felt the rumble of thousands of legionnaires galloping behind him. He looked to his right and watched Winston springing through the grass. He looked up. His flag snapped in the wind. He looked over his shoulder behind him.

He finally saw what his dream never revealed.

The guardians of God's gift—thousands of them.

Something changed inside Fletcher. Something was different. A peace that he has never felt filled his heart. His soul calmed as he charged towards war.

A new vision flooded into Fletcher's mind as he raced down the hill towards the Anics.

It was a vision that didn't taunt. It didn't perplex.

He welcomed the vision. It was a dream that Fletcher hoped and waited for.

He envisioned Sofia sitting in an orchard under an apple tree with two young boys and a girl. An aged and shaggy Winston rested at their feet. One of the boys petted the old spaniel. Fletcher's mother leaned against Willard in the shade. Willard looked content in his sunset years as he proudly told stories of Crassius and Servius to his grandchildren. Captivation radiated from their youthful eyes as they experienced the same freedom that their parents and grandparents enjoyed.

The honeyfield.

Fletcher closed his eyes.

Thank you, God.

Dedication

This book is dedicated to the 1.2 million Americans who sacrificed their lives during the Revolutionary War, Civil War, WWI, WWII, Korean War, Vietnam War, Iraq, Afghanistan and all other conflicts in foreign and unfriendly lands to protect and preserve the Constitution of the United States.

This book is dedicated to all police officers and law enforcement agents who have nobly dedicated their careers and for some, their lives, protecting Americans and their families from domestic evil.

America's guardians enabled the first nation in history to shelter God's gift of divine energy in each of us.

Previous generations of Americans handed a strong and free country to their children and to us. Today, our military and local police are protecting the nation that we hope to hand to our children. We sleep peacefully at night because of these great men and women. They are the true guardians of our life, liberty, and pursuit of happiness.

Finally, this book is dedicated to the Founding Fathers of the greatest nation known to mankind. Without their courage, sacrifice, unyielding belief in divine providence, and selfless devotion to protecting freedom for their posterity, the world would be a very different and darker place today.

www.ingramcontent.com/pod-product-compliance
Lightning Source LLC
Chambersburg PA
CBHW071717140626
46557CB00012B/880